I0458051

THE COURTING

BENJAMIN CARD

Villipede Publications
PO Box 3643
Idaho Falls, ID 83403
villipede.com

Special discounts are available on quantity purchases by
corporations, associations, and others. For details, contact the
publisher at the address above.

Printed in the United States of America

ISBN-13: 978-0692262481
ISBN-10: 0692262482

First Edition

The stories "Wake Up!" and "I'll Spend It With You" first
published by Grey Gecko Press (greygeckopress.com); reprinted
herein with permission.

For my brother Abe

Thanks for showing me
that there is still happiness to be found
even in the darkest corners of life.

◖ Acknowledgments

I'd like to first thank God, because he's clearly responsible for stirring the embers in this weird brain of mine. Thanks to my massive family: Gabriel, Josue, Dan (aka Mr. Hublot, aka Sleazy Chester Chestnut, aka Henry Humphries, aka Cecil Evergreen, aka Inspector Stanton Keeshof [he inspects toenails for bacteria]), Pete, Abe, Sam, Jessi, Nicky, Joey, Ruben, Ismy, Oscar, Kevin, Big Serp, Lisi, Jackie, and Emily, and all the older folks in the family. My parents, Lidia, Luis, Eddie, and Nelsy, for always being there for me and never letting me hit rock bottom. And to Pedro and Sonia, who are basically like parents to me. Thanks to my best friends: David, Jenise, and Manny. A special thanks to Kendare Blake, for reading my stories and putting up with all my stalkerish Facebook messages.

Sometimes I think I'm schizophrenic and I made up all these awesome people in my life. Then I get creeped out and think about something else.

Thanks to all of you in my life. If I forgot to mention your name, I'm sorry. That speaks more of my bad memory than of your importance. I love you all. This first one's for you.

—Benjamin Card, 2014

◖ Foreword

From an early age I was surrounded by books and encouraged to embrace the love of literacy. My father Robert was one of the foremost experts in commercial aviation history and my uncle created one of the most famous and still-relevant science fiction television shows in history, The Twilight Zone. While my tastes tend to run towards the medical and scientific realm, albeit with a dash of weekend romance novels thrown in, there is something to be said about a good science fiction story. I was approached by Benjamin to read "The Courting" and it didn't take much to convince me it was worth a look. From the first glance at the cover, it reminded me of the mysteries I would see gathering space on my Dad's and Uncle Rod's bookshelves. I started reading it one afternoon this past weekend and was immediately transported into something reminiscent of a Twilight Zone episode. I could very easily picture the chaos of women standing in the streets with their eyes towards the heavens and feel the anger and frustration that the men of the world were dealing with. Benjamin has a gift for allowing the reader to visualize the story in their own minds; which can be a challenge in the electronic-focused world today, which tends to squelch the imagination.

Throughout their careers, my father and uncle were frequently asked to read up-and-coming manuscripts and give advice to young authors. I was always told by my dad how difficult it was to make a living from writing stories. Yet, as challenging as it was at times, it was his life's passion, which continued right up until his death at 92. Benjamin's writing shows that same passion and commitment to the age old tradition of story telling.

—Jennifer Serling
August 4, 2014

◖ The Courting

ANGELO OPENED ONE LAST PACK of sugar and tipped it over his coffee. He never used this much sugar, but in the last week he hadn't been sleeping very well and needed the energy. Neither had Kimberly, his wife. They were too busy being up, fighting all the time. And when they finally would slip into bed together, it was like two warring soldiers sharing the same rifle. Eventually—last night—Angelo took the hint and made his bed on the couch downstairs. It was colder down there—the heater had to work for a much larger space on the first floor— but he could sleep better with cold skin than beside a cold heart.

He watched the coffee's surface puff up as he stirred the sugar that settled. It made a foamy sound that he couldn't quite hear, but that he imagined vividly as the minuscule bubbles formed and popped rapidly. Tossing the spoon into the sink, he lifted the mug and walked over to the window.

Jesus, he thought. *Talk about being dramatic.* Kimberly, since 6 a.m., had been sitting on an empty parking space bumper outside their house. It was almost 8 a.m. now. She was never up before 9 a.m.

Let her do what she wants, he thought bitterly. *Let her starve out there. It's her bidding. See if I give a damn.* He felt almost instantly guilty for thinking that way; but in the four years of their marriage, he had never seen her get this upset over nothing. He couldn't even remember what they were fighting about.

He sipped at the coffee, and winced as the blinding fire burned his lips.

"*Dammit*," he muttered, licking his teeth to cool his tongue.

Alright, he thought, superstitiously thinking that the burn was a sign from some deity above. *Alright, I'll offer her some breakfast.* That route always worked. They'd argue, and he'd clean up the mess by doing a good deed for her. Something to surprise her; catch her off guard. Last fight, only a few weeks ago, he'd cleaned the entire house before she was out of bed. He was too tired to do that now, so he hoped a nice and simple breakfast would do the trick.

Inspired, he moved to the fridge and brought out the eggs, bacon, and toast. First, he heated up the pan and started to fry the eggs. *Kim likes hers sunny-side up*, he thought with satisfaction. Then he put the two bacon strips in the microwave. Toast in the toaster was last.

About five minutes later, breakfast was ready on a shiny white porcelain plate. Record time! The platter glowed, it seemed, and the soft, inviting smell permeated the air. Holding the plate, he rolled the knob of the front door and stepped outside.

Kimberly was still on the parking bumper, as he expected. She was looking up at the sky. There were a few clouds, but they were scattered about like melting marshmallows in a cup of hot chocolate.

"Kim?" Angelo called.

She didn't react, only continued to gaze upward.

"Kim, please," he said, beginning to feel ridiculous for making breakfast without asking her first. He looked down at his plate; it was getting cold in the November air, he could feel it.

"Baby," he tried again. "I made you breakfast. Will you please come inside?"

There, he thought. *That should do the trick.* He sounded completely vulnerable; she had to hear it in his voice.

Still, she didn't respond. She didn't even twitch a muscle. Aside from her brown hair waving in the wind, she was completely still.

This is ridiculous, he thought. *She's taken this whole thing too far, too damn far!* He slammed the front door and dropped the plate of food into the sink. It crashed and scattered madly. Turning, he glanced outside again, to see if Kimberly had noticed his reaction. If she had, she hid the fact well. *Dammit*, he thought again. He wasn't going to let it bother him.

Angelo began heading past the kitchen for the stairs, then stopped. He glanced above the refrigerator and saw the half-empty bottle of gin. *It's too early for that*, his mind offered. His fingers involuntarily twitched when he saw the rack of empty glasses.

Just one glass, he thought. *I can't take her shit anymore. At least not sober.*

He walked over to the gin, pulled it from atop the fridge, and poured himself a glass. He'd forgotten to make ice the last time.

"Screw it," he mumbled.

He took the glass with him upstairs and shut the bedroom door. Sipped at the tangy, burning gin until it was gone.

Then he fell asleep.

◖

HE AWOKE WITH A START. Confused, he gazed around with blurry vision, wondering if this was the first time he'd woken up today. Then he saw the empty glass. He leaned over to look at the digital clock hanging across the room—9 a.m.

Work in an hour.

He heard thunder outside; it made the window tremble slightly. It was raining. Not hard, but no drizzle either. Kimberly worked at 10 a.m. also, at a daycare just two miles from their home. Angelo worked at Jim Bell's Auto Repair, a small shop just off the Palmetto Expressway. Kimberly should be gone by now.

Angelo felt a cavernous pain in his stomach and thought about food. He should have eaten that breakfast himself instead of foolishly tossing it in the sink. But he wanted Kimberly to see the mess later, so that she would know how angry he'd been.

He got up. There wasn't time to shower, so he went over to the closet and picked out his clothes. Black pants, white pin-stripe shirt, black tie. And the same dress shoes he always wore.

He got dressed and walked into the bathroom that connected to their bedroom. He turned on the light, brushed his teeth, and styled his longish black hair. He hated the smell the hair gel left on his fingers, but he didn't have time to wash it off thoroughly. Instead, he wiped the residue on the surface of his pants.

Once downstairs, he grabbed a banana from the kitchen and peeled it. He ate it quickly. He would eat something from the vending machine at work. He almost walked outside before remembering the rain.

Umbrella, umbrella, he thought, peering around the room. He found an umbrella wedged between the fridge and the oven, and snagged it. It must've not been raining when Kimberly left the house.

She hadn't bothered to touch the mess he left in the sink, either. Grunting, he opened the front door. He heard the symphonic clapping of rain on cement and knew he couldn't make it to the car without using the umbrella. He opened it, then lifted it over his head.

Then he saw Kimberly. Still sitting on the parking bumper, staring up at the sky with arms outstretched.

It was the beginning.

◀ Two

BEFORE HE EVEN HAD TIME to feel anger, Angelo felt a hideous fear for her life. What the hell was she thinking?

"Kimberly!" he shouted over the trampling rain.

She didn't move. He marched over with the umbrella shielding most of him, unable to escape the rain that was swept up by the wind. Kimberly was completely soaked in her nightgown. *She's going to catch pneumonia*, he thought in near panic. He tried to guard her with the umbrella, but it was difficult from her sitting position. He would have to sit with her and wet all his clothes.

"Kim! What the hell is wrong with you! Are you insane?" he yelled. "Get your ass back in the house, now!"

She looked up at him coldly. "Will you move that umbrella? You're blocking my view."

Angelo could barely hear her over the rain. Had she really said what he thought she had? His face was a mask of disbelief and anger. He grabbed her violently by the arm and began to tug at her to get her to stand. She fought him.

"What are you doing?" she yelled. "You're hurting me!"

"I don't care! You're going to die out here!"

Right after he said it, the rain began to thin out until, within a matter of fifteen seconds, it stopped completely. Angelo lowered the umbrella and looked up. The gray clouds in the sky had scattered, and the morning sun was reaching them, crowning the edges of the clouds with gold and silver linings.

He looked back down at Kimberly.

She gave him a smug look, puckering her lips at him with brute accomplishment.

He took a step back. *What is happening?* he thought. *This isn't happening.*

He closed the umbrella and reentered the house. He wedged it angrily between the fridge and oven again, then turned to go outside.

He tried not to look at her. He made a beeline for his car, which was two empty parking spaces beside her. Through the corner of his eye, he could still see her sitting there, soaked and wavering from side to side, as if to the melody of a song.

He ignored it. He had to get to work.

Numbly, he opened the door of his car and sat inside. *What on earth is happening?* he thought again. Had his wife gone insane? There was no other explanation.

He glanced quickly to the side, only to get a glimpse of her through his tinted windows. Kimberly was giggling alone, still gazing upward, her shoulders clambered up towards her chin.

Dazedly, Angelo turned on the car and rolled it back. He began driving off, out of his neighborhood.

What was she thinking? he thought again. *What could have caused her to act this way? Maybe she—*

"Jesus!" he screamed, jerking the car hard to the right.

A woman had carelessly stepped in front of the car, moving clumsily along the street. Angelo almost hit her, and almost hit a parked car when he swerved. But luckily, he turned and braked in time to avoid both accidents. He held a button to lower the window.

"Ma'am, are you alright?" he said, his heart pounding in his chest. "You gotta be careful. I almost got you."

The blonde woman—in her mid-thirties—was a neighbor about four houses down from his. He'd seen her throw out the trash some mornings. She was attractive; and he remembered thinking so at some point in the past. This morning she had no trash, and she was still in her pajamas.

She seemed to be looking around for something in the sky as an airplane went blaring by.

"Are you okay?" Angelo asked, resting his elbow on the door.

She was mumbling something and laughing, but it was impossible to hear her.

"Well, look . . ." he started. "I gotta head off to work. Again, I'm really sorry. But you do gotta be more careful next time. Alright? Okay, I'll see you later. I live—" He glanced back at his house. He couldn't see Kim from his position, and hoped to God she wasn't still there.

Turning forward again, he offered the blonde woman an awkward wave good-bye and drove off. It didn't take long, though.

Even before leaving his block, it didn't take long for him to notice the dozens of women loitering along the street, all of them gazing upward to the sky, all of them with inexplicable grins on their faces. And some with husbands, like Angelo, trying to snap them back to reality.

◀ Three

ANGELO'S FIRST ANCHORING THOUGHT was that he still had to get to work. But as he glanced at the rear-view mirror, unable to catch sight of Kimberly, he knew that he couldn't leave her alone. He weaved around the obstacle course of women—some of them only gazing upward, some dancing or reaching up with their hands. There were some men out there too; maybe about half the amount of women. And they looked as terrified as Angelo felt. He turned a sharp right and clutched his cell phone.

He dialed his boss. The line was busy.

He tried again. It rang this time. Angelo heard the dull click as the phone was answered.

"Hello?" said Mr. Hans, his boss.

"Hey, it's Angelo," he said. "I don't think I'll be able to make it to the shop today. Can you manage without me? It's kind of urgent."

Angelo made another right turn, making a second round back to his block. As his car straightened into the adjacent block, he saw about another dozen women outside, frolicking through the streets, some with their husbands chasing behind.

"Jesus," Mr. Hans said. Through the static noise of the phone, it sounded like Hans was sobbing. "What the hell is going on out there, Angelo? Do you know what could be causing this?"

"What do you mean?" Angelo said, feeling a resonant shock of panic in his chest.

"It's the same everywhere." The man was definitely crying. Angelo could almost feel his boss's sobbing breath through the phone's speaker.

"Jesus, this is happening everywhere?"

"Yeah, it's—" Hans's voice broke off. "Honey! Honey sit back—" And the line cut off.

Angelo lowered the phone just as he reached his house again. His fingertips were trembling slightly, and he dazedly turned the car into the pocket of its parking space.

Looking out the window, he saw an oblivious Kimberly swaying, nearly swooning, atop the parking bumper beside him. Her smile was broad, and she was mumbling something indistinct.

Angelo exited the car and shut the door, feeling nothing but a stiffness in his veins, his colorless face void of any real consciousness. He approached Kimberly slowly, aware of the dozens of shouting voices around him, filling the streets with confused panic.

"Baby?" he tried. "Are you okay? Do you want to go inside with me?"

She chuckled. "No. Don't call me that. Don't call me that. I belong to someone else."

And then she craned her neck back and peered up at the grayish-blue sky.

"I love you," Kimberly said softly. But not to Angelo. Her eyes were fixed on the sky.

ANGELO SAT IN THE KITCHEN, trying the phone again. He must have tried at least eighteen times—calling his mother's cell, his brother's, his father-in-law's—always the busy tone. This must have really been happening everywhere. Giving up, he hooked the phone onto its cradle and rose from the stool.

The news, he thought suddenly.

He almost hurdled towards the television and scooped up the remote which sat atop it. He pressed the ON button and the TV beamed to life. He didn't have to switch to the news station—this phenomenon was being reported on every channel. ". . . the exact time of the occurrence. Some are guessing it took place sometime between 5 and 6 a.m. Others claim it began much earlier, but the signs were milder. As the hours go by, we're beginning to notice the action of these women intensify."

The heading of the story read—Women On Strike Worldwide?

Worldwide? A helpless feeling blossomed in Angelo, blooming in a smoky cold pit in his stomach. How could this be worldwide? What was happening?

He lowered the volume and instinctively began pacing the room. He heard the muffled noise outside growing louder; an odd mixture of laughing and angry yelling. The laughing coming from the women, the yelling from the men. None of it made sense. And though he knew that Kim needed him, he was honestly terrified to see her again. That face, that mysterious grin. Those loving eyes. Loving on what? On whom? There was nothing up there. Only sky.

It was then that Angelo heard a gunshot. He'd never heard one in real life, but it had to be a gun. His heart throbbed violently in his chest and he ducked, feeling his knees catch his weight just before he was on the ground.

His ears rang slightly, and he could only hear his labored breathing for a moment. Then, after a moment, he heard a man screaming, crying out in pain.

Angelo crawled to the window and peered out. It was the couple across from his house. The man lay on the street in a bloody puddle, which bubbled over the hot cement. He stopped squirming suddenly. The woman, the man's wife, held the gun. She mumbled something funny to herself and slipped it back into her pajama pants.

Angelo felt his knees crash to the floor before he even noticed they dropped. His heart was a hammering cyclone in his chest, sending alarming signals to every part of his body. He turned hastily, feeling his brain and his body move at different intervals. Before he knew it, he was pacing and bending his way around the kitchen, to the front door.

Kimberly. That was the only thing on his mind at that moment. He found that truth incredibly heroic and incredibly stupid.

He pinched open the front door, slowly and carefully. A gunshot, his mind framed the situation. He'd never heard a gunshot in his life. Well, that wasn't true. One time when he'd gone to the range with his older brother.

But that was at least ten years ago. No—that was an entirely different thing. This was his neighbor; he'd been shot. *Oh my god*, Angelo thought as reality sank in. *Someone died in front of my house. And what's worse. Kim is out there.*

He stumbled outside, feeling half-caught in a dream. When he passed the newly-painted wooden fence only a few feet beyond, he saw the parking lot and Kimberly standing idly to the side. Her brown hair covered her face.

But that wasn't the first thing Angelo noticed. The first was the dead man on the ground; his blood carpeted beneath him, exhausted in a dry red shadow.

It felt like a long time before he reached Kim's side.

"Now! Inside!" he yelled, grabbing her.

She fought it, but he was stronger than her.

"That's right!" the woman across the street yelled; the one who'd shot her husband. "Take 'er on back inside."

Angelo jerked his head back, but only to see if the woman had drawn her gun. She hadn't. He continued, tugging at his wife.

"What do you think you're—" Kimberly roared, in a tone he'd never heard her speak. Like an angry cat; a loud screech erupting from her throat.

He shoved her into the house, then leaned against the counter, amazed at how much energy he'd exerted. Kimberly rose from the ground, then started for the door. Angelo blocked her path.

"No, Kim," he said. "You're not going back out there."

"Get the fuck out of my way." She spat the words out, so fruitfully that he felt a sloppy spray of saliva fan his face.

"I will not," he answered her. When had she ever spoken to him this way? "Go to your room," he ordered.

"I'm not a child," she hissed. "Now move before I hurt you."

She was weaker than he, yes. But the way she said it made fear bubble up inside of him. Her confidence was unmistakable.

Her eyes flickered across the counter and she snatched a lone butter knife. There was still butter and syrup caked on it from the breakfast he'd made earlier.

"What are you doing? Put that down," he said.

She smiled slowly. But it wasn't a cheerful smile; it was the smile one cracked when told a useful secret. The secret that they had the upper hand now. Her eyes became narrow slits.

"Move," she said thinly.

Angelo wanted to say no; he wanted to, but he kept eyeing the knife, and the way her forearm muscles flexed behind it. She wasn't bluffing. She would use it if she had to. The realization terrified him, and he moved against the counter, clearing the path for her.

Kimberly brushed past him carelessly, dropping the knife as soon as she reached the parking lot. Her head shifted to the sky again.

◀ Four

ANGELO RECOVERED THE KNIFE and held it over the sink.

"No," he mumbled.

Turning quickly, he opened the cabinets and recovered every utensil and sharp object in the kitchen, then carried them in sloppy bundles to the living room. He hid them in a drawer in the pantry closet—a few forks and knifes had fallen along the way and he retraced to recover them.

Once the kitchen felt safe, he did the same for the rest of the first floor. Things he thought she could use as a weapon—a couple of small metal picture frames, a small lamp, a few other things and finally, the umbrella.

When he was finished, he sat down tiredly on the couch in the living room. His eyes burned in front of him at nothing in particular, noticing that the room looked a little emptier. He remained sitting there for at least fifteen minutes, then forced himself to stand. He walked back outside.

She was still there. The noise in the streets was quieter now, and Angelo didn't know why. Perhaps the men had given up. *Or maybe they were all killed*, came the chilling thought.

"No, no," he said, shaking his head.

He passed the lawn fence and saw Kimberly sitting on the parking bump, her shoulders relaxed. He couldn't see her face; she had her back to him. He stepped closer, slowly, cautiously, feeling his legs move stiffly like each leg was lifting and dropping heavy luggage.

And then he sat beside her. She didn't even seem to acknowledge his presence.

His throat quivered. "Hey," he said. It came out sounding more forceful than he'd hoped, but she definitely heard him.

She took a quick one-second glance at him and looked away. "Umm . . . hi," she said.

Angelo wanted to run away. This was too strange for him, too bizarre. It was too horrific to be treated like a stranger by his own wife. His fingers dug anxiously into his knees.

"What . . ." he started, then swallowed. "How are you feeling?"

This time, she took a moment to answer. She turned her face to him and her lips relaxed into a soft smile. "I'm doing . . ." she started, ". . . fantastic."

"Oh," Angelo said. "That's good then."

He heard buzzing and looked up to see a swarm of mosquitoes zipping over the dead man's body; his neighbor. The man's wife was still there too, smiling and swaying from side to side. Angelo felt bile rise up in his throat, and his face became pale. "Oh God," he croaked. "I'm gonna throw up."

Kimberly ignored his comment.

Angelo rose abruptly and rushed into the house. He hung his head over the sink and grunted. His vision felt skewed, as if he were looking at the faucet through lenses too thick, lenses on glasses designed for an elderly man.

He gagged. Then gagged again, and again, each time more watery than the last.

Then he vomited a hot stinky soup of bile, right over the breakfast he'd cooked earlier that morning.

Angelo heard a knock on the door. His head whipped to the side, thinking for a hopeful moment that it was his wife. Through the window, he saw a tan Hispanic man breathing heavily. His eyes were so bloated that Angelo thought they might slip right out their sockets.

"Open up, man!" the man said behind the glass. "I'm not dangerous."

Angelo recognized the man. He lived somewhere on the same block, but Angelo couldn't remember where.

"You deaf?" the man shouted, his buggy eyes growing larger by the second.

Angelo looked down at the bile in the sink and then over at the man. The man was short; his face hardly reached over the door's window, making him no more than 5'6". Angelo couldn't see his body, though, only his face. But since his face was chubby, Angelo predicted that the rest of him would be chubby as well.

"I got it," Angelo said at last, hurrying for the door.

When he opened it, the man nearly tumbled inside. He was sweating and panting, dabbing at the beads of sweat on his face; they first looked like pimples before he rubbed them away.

"Water, please man," the short chubby Hispanic man said, hovering over the fridge like a dog waiting to be fed.

"Of course," Angelo said.

Angelo grabbed a nearby clean mug and filled it with cold water from the fridge. Almost as he was handing it over, the man was already drinking it. And it was gone in one relentless swallow.

"More," the man said, this time not bothering to say please.

This happened two more times before he put the mug down on the counter and sat himself on one of the kitchen stools.

"Is that your girl out there?" he asked.

"My wife," Angelo said.

The man nodded.

"So this shit's really everywhere, huh?"

Angelo shrugged, but he caught himself nodding too.

"I live just down the block," the man said. "Over near the playground." He shook his head slowly. "You'll be smelling the place pretty soon. What's left of it."

"Smelling?"

"My sister burned it up. She just . . ." he closed his fists and flicked them open, raising them higher. "Poof."

"I'm sorry," Angelo said, because he didn't know what else to say. Did this man expect to live here now? The whole situation was odd.

As if reading his mind, the man said: "Oh . . . how rude of me. My name is Felix. Felix Solaris." He held out his hand for Angelo to shake.

Angelo took it. "Angelo," he said.

The man nodded, smiling subjectively.

"Nice place you got here, Angelo."

"Thanks."

His face melted into a frown. "My fucking house . . ." he said, then gave a regretful wave of his hand. "Pardon my French."

"It's fine," Angelo said. "You wanna sit down?" They both sat on the couch in the kitchen near the television set. It was off, but Angelo could only imagine what was playing on the news. Chaos, to be sure. Madness.

Madness, he thought. But why? What on earth was happening? Angelo looked at Felix who was fiddling with his umpteenth glass of water.

"What . . ." Angelo started. "What the fuck is going on out there?" Then he added, "I speak French, too."

Felix gave a sad smile. "I wish I knew, man . . . I wish I knew."

Angelo sighed. "You want a drink? I've got some gin. Or scotch."

He sat up straighter and slapped his hands to his knees. "You found my kryptonite. Gin it is."

"On the rocks okay?"

Felix nodded. "Only on special occasions. I think today qualifies."

Angelo got up and fished out two small glasses from one of the upper shelves in the kitchen. The refrigerator pumped out cubes of ice which crashed into the glasses. Then he poured the gin. There was only enough for one full glass each. If Felix wanted more, he would have to settle for scotch.

"Here you go," Angelo said, handing Felix the drink.

"Ahh . . ." he said. "Too kind, too kind."

Angelo took a seat. "You seem to be holding up pretty well for someone who just lost his house."

Felix lowered the glass from his lips. They formed a tight line as he swallowed the gin. "Let's not make this about me. Okay?"

Angelo was silent, so Felix went on. "The whole world's gonna lose a lot more than their home today. You saw that neighbor of yours dead in the street, right? Yeah—I doubt he's the only casualty. Those women out there—they're deranged. Whatever this is, it's big. I've come to terms with that. Maybe you should, too. Yeah, I lost my fucking house, but at least I didn't lose my mind like those fucking idiotic men out there. They're gonna get themselves killed if they keep trying to reason with those lunatics." He lifted up his empty glass.

Angelo took it. "I only have whiskey left."

"My new best friend."

Angelo wasn't sure if he was referring to him or the scotch. He went to wash and refill the glass. Felix continued talking from the other room.

"So," he called out. "Do you have a plan or do you think we should just wait this out?"

The way he said 'we' made Angelo's shoulders slump. He had enough on his hands with Kimberly, he didn't need to babysit this grown man right now.

"No plan," Angelo called back. "I'm just focused on my wife right now."

He was hoping Felix would get the point. Angelo, though, had a feeling it wouldn't be that easy. He returned to the living room, handed Felix the drink.

"Thanks, kind sir," he said, taking it. It went straight to his lips. "I hear you, though. About your wife. Must be scary shit. I'm single, thank God."

"What about your sister?" Angelo asked, gently swirling his drink but not particularly wanting to drink too much in the company of this man.

"She's single, too," he said quickly.

"No," Angelo said. "I mean, aren't you scared for her, too?"

Felix rubbed his fat hands over his thighs. Then his face became somber. "Of course, man. But I'm scared. I'm scared of seeing her again. And now I can't even go inside my house."

"Do you have—family that maybe—?" Angelo inquired.

"Hey, man, I get it," Felix said, setting down his drink and getting up. "I'm sure I've overstayed my welcome. Thanks for the drinks, though."

Angelo, throughout, was wagging his head like he was appalled by the notion, but inside, he was glad that the man had finally taken the hint. He didn't have time for relaxation and small talk. Not with Kim still out there. Felix reached the front door, and turned to shake Angelo's hand.

"Thanks again," he said. "I mean that."

Angelo shook his hand. "Where are you going?"

"I don't know," he said. "Maybe for a drive."

He released his grip on him and watched him go. Felix nodded a sad greeting to Kimberly as he crossed the block.

◖

ANGELO WAS ALONE AGAIN. He was glad for it. He needed time to think, to devise a plan. Felix was a nice guy, sure—albeit strange in some ways—but he was also a major distraction. If Angelo hadn't spoken up, surely they'd still be rooted to the couch, drinking the last puddle of scotch and telling old war stories. It wasn't progress. Angelo needed his wife back. He didn't care that this was happening everywhere. It was happening here. To Kim. That's what mattered.

Maybe they found something out on the news, he thought suddenly.

He went over to the living room and clicked on the television.

"—are still trying to find the cause of this. All we know for sure is that these women are suffering from a serious chemical imbalance in the brain and are dangerous because of it. So far, over six-hundred people reported dead to the authorities. Thousands injured. In the U.S. alone."

Jesus, Angelo thought, sinking further back into the couch. He rubbed his scruffy beard—partly to make sure he wasn't dreaming.

"Reports on some of the women tested show an excessive increase in dopamine, norepinephrine, and slightly higher levels of oxytocin. These are all chemicals that stimulate feelings of love and affection, and also adrenaline. How these levels were induced, we have yet to know. For some reason, it has affected only women and has come from an unknown source."

Angelo muted the TV while the man went on talking.

An unknown source, he thought, sinking ever-deeper into the couch. *Their love is too large now. Too large to pour out to another man . . .*

So they love on the vast sky.

◀ FIVE

AN IDEA OCCURRED TO ANGELO later that evening, as he watched Kimberly from the bedroom window upstairs. He could see two rows of women on the street, though some were hardly visible in the lamplight; walking in circles or rocking their hips slowly, shifting in and out of Angelo's view.

The idea was this: maybe Angelo could redirect Kimberly's affection back to himself. True, he didn't quite know the intensity of her love, and this plan could easily backfire; but to him, any plan deserved a chance. He had to try it.

He couldn't wait till morning. So that evening, he stumbled downstairs and went outside his house. He stood beside Kim in the cold-wrapped night, stuffed his hands into his pockets, and sighed.

"Cold night," he said. It felt strange to induce small talk as if Kimberly was a complete stranger.

"Oh, yes it is," Kim said, her eyes darting to him briefly and then flitting away.

"So—" Angelo felt weird for going this direction in the conversation, but he had already planned this for hours before, and he wasn't about to quit so soon, "—are you seeing anyone?"

He could tell that Kimberly was taken aback by his sudden approach. She seemed to shrivel away in the dark.

"Well, aren't you fresh," she said, her voice ladened with discomfort. "I'm sorry," Angelo said. "You're just a pretty girl and I—"

"Enough of that," she said quickly, though her voice still trembled slightly. Angelo couldn't tell if it was because of the cold or her fear. He decided not to dwell on it and continued prying.

"So tell me about . . ."

"My love?" she said too quickly, boldly.

"Yes." Angelo cringed.

"He's everything I've ever wanted. He's my soul mate; I know it for a fact. He's," she began to smile, her eyes shining brighter than the lamps overhead, "just perfect."

"Well, where is he?" Angelo inquired, growing frustrated.

Kimberly raised her eyebrows at him, as if he'd asked the stupidest question that ever was asked. "Can't you look up?" she said scornfully.

Angelo looked up. "I see the sky. Just cold, black expanse."

"Enough," she said sharply.

"Cloudy, starless—"

"I said enough!" she roared, slapping Angelo hard across the face.

He stumbled back, a sharp pain like concentrated fire biting his cheek, exploding in his head. He could see her eyebrows twitching with anger, her teeth exposed and knit together tightly. She was clenching them so hard that Angelo thought he could actually see them sinking slowly into her gums.

He held up his arms to keep a distance between them. Between he and his wife.

"Okay," he said. "I'm going inside now."

"Good," she said shakily. "Go and don't ever come back."

◖

HE MADE AN ATTEMPT TO SLEEP. In his room, Angelo could hear noises that he was not accustomed to hearing this late at night. He was sprawled across his bed, drunk off whiskey. He had drunk the remaining half of the bottle that was in the kitchen. He lay watching the fan swirl in rhythmic circles overhead, in the dark, and it sounded like a lazy helicopter descending. Angelo wondered if the blades of the fan could falter and fall on top of him, crushing his face in. With each spin, the center of the fan would wobble. Like a loose screw cringing under too much weight.

But the sounds outside earned the majority of his attention: laughs, wails, sexual sounds. Praises, songs, words of adoration.

Through the muffled glass, he could hear his wife below in the parking lot.

"I loveee you!" she was shouting. Her tone was so intense that it almost sounded like she was weeping. "Thank youuu! You're my *everything*. My whole world."

Angelo listened numbly, his ears hot and ringing with drunken intensity.

"My soul, my song!" his wife said, her voice scratchy with exhausted passion. "Never leave, never go. Never go!"

And then the numbness veered him to blackout sleep.

◀ SIX

HIS HEAD WAS THROBBING in the morning. He had to shut off the fan quickly, because even the sight of the blades spinning sent throbs of lightning to his temples. He hobbled downstairs, feeling an inflated ache in his heels.

Today is the day, he thought. *Today I'll force her inside. Today I'll make her come to her senses, whether she likes it or not.*

He didn't bother making breakfast. He started straight away with his plan, and it was this: he would—somehow, as quickly and painlessly as he could—get her unconscious, then tie her up and bring her inside. He would then tie her to the bed (*like an exorcism*, the chilling thought came) and break her the way one broke an untamed horse. He would force words out of her. Squeeze out more information than the television could give. The plan made him sick to his stomach—to have to force his wife to do anything made him feel nauseated—but if he wanted to save Kimberly, he had no choice.

He retrieved nylon rope from the garage—just enough to tie the arms and legs—then went into the kitchen. He didn't know how he would control her. Sure, he was much stronger than she was. But these were abnormal circumstances. She had strength fueled by this fervid drug now; a power that was primitive and almost supernatural. It was inspired and passionate, and that made her stronger than Angelo.

He would find a way. If it came down to violence, he would show some if it meant keeping her safe. And that was probably what it would come down to.

Angelo stepped outside into the cool morning air. It would be a beautiful day . . . if the streets weren't littered with dozens of hysterical women; if there wasn't a rotting dead man strewn on the gravel; if Angelo's wife wasn't estranged.

There she was—sitting this time, which would make it harder for him to suppress her.

Still, somehow, he would get the job done. He approached her, raising the rope in one shaky arm with a clammy hand gripping it tightly. His free hand was wagging around purposelessly, then he raised it over her shoulder.

Kimberly's head whipped back.

"What—" she started to say, but Angelo was already on her, jostling her to the hard ground and forcing her arms down. She was too strong. Not too strong to hold down, but too strong to suppress while tying the rope to her arms and legs.

"Get 'er outta hereee," the woman across the street yelled, laughing triumphantly and clapping her hands.

Angelo ignored her as he continued to wrestle his wife.

"Let me— let me, lemme!—" she hollered, her neck twisting in almost impossible angles.

Angelo didn't have a choice; he raised his arm and struck his fist hard against her jaw. So hard that her head dribbled once off the pavement like a basketball. Then her body went limp.

"Ah—No!" he cried, looking around shakily, almost expecting to see someone staring in disbelieving shock at what he'd done. Nobody stared. The men—the women, of course, were too preoccupied in their delusion to ever notice a thing—who were outside were too busy handling (or mishandling) their wives, sisters, mothers, lovers.

He looked back to his wife. That he'd hit her, struck her—he couldn't believe it. There was a fresh grid of bloody scratches on her forehead. The sight made him sick. But it was necessary, a voice reminded him. He checked her pulse because he was afraid he'd killed her accidentally. She was alive.

After he tied her arms and legs, he carried her into the house. Then through the kitchen. Then through the living room. Then upstairs. Then to bed. He must have stopped at least a dozen times, and each time terrified that she would wake up—especially while ascending the stairs—and put up another fight. He couldn't imagine hitting her like that again.

Once she was laid out on the bed, Angelo stood a distance, panting and staring. He pulled up the computer chair at the corner of the room and placed it directly in front of the bed. He waited, with equal parts patience and anxiety revolving swiftly in his mind. His hand twitched when she finally woke up.

She looked around dizzily, and for a dumb moment Angelo thought she was back to her normal self. That moment passed too soon when she focused her eyes on him appallingly.

"You!" she hissed.

"Stay calm—" he started, as she began screaming blindly over him. "I need you to calm down so I can—"

"You bitch! I'll kill you. He'll kill you!" That stopped Angelo in his speech. He swallowed dryly and leaned up in his chair.

"Who?" he said. "Who will?"

She smiled in that 'I-know-a-secret-you-don't' way again, and Angelo numbly sat back. The pallid morning light planted new features on her face, features that scared Angelo to his bones. Features he'd never seen on his wife's face in the past; on anyone's face, for that matter, except in old horror movies.

"My . . . Love," she said introspectively.

Angelo swallowed again, trying to do it without her noticing; that, too, was as futile as trying to eat a whole fruit without biting into it.

"Yeah, well what the hell does that mean?" he snapped.

She looked out the window. Her face became somber. Angelo could actually see her chest rise and fall with each breath, and he could almost imagine her ribs pushing up against her pale skin. He followed her gaze to the window and grunted. Getting up, he went to the window and swung the drapes closed. The room suddenly became dipped in darkness. And with the darkness, came Kimberly's sudden cries.

"No!" she screamed, a writhing shadow in the dark.

"You're going to tell me what I want to know, Kim," Angelo said.

"I'll tell you nothing! I'll never betray my Love!"

Angelo sat again and pressed his thumbs to his forehead.

"I just want to know what's going on."

There was a moment's silence, and Angelo thought that perhaps—finally!—she was coming back to her senses. But when, he wondered shortly after, would he stop being so naïve?

No, she was silent because she was weeping. He heard her quiet, mucus-laden sobs in the dark, seeing that same shadowy figure of hers shiver in the murky grayness of the room. He couldn't stand seeing her this way; it was a branding iron against his heart.

Soon her weeping was stifled to a low wheezing. And then, a long while after that, she had passed out from fatigue. His plan had failed irrefutably.

Angelo rose, untied her arms and legs, and carried her back downstairs and out into the sad street where she— falsely—felt happiest.

◖

ANGELO WALKED OFF a few blocks after leaving Kimberly at the parking bumper. He hid his hands in his pockets. He needed to go for a walk. He had to think all of this through; figure out a new way to reach his wife. He tried to think about the world in its current state—a world where women no longer sought the comfort of men, no longer needed their help for anything at all. This drug, whatever it was, supplied them with all that. And a world where men could never again earn the love of a woman. Unless taking it by force.

Angelo had been walking almost without realizing it. At the end of their confined neighborhood, he saw a man serenading his wife (presumably his wife, but it could've just as easily been his girlfriend or fiancée or anyone else, for that matter). He was standing comically in front of her with an acoustic nylon-stringed guitar hugging his chest. The sound rang sweetly in the air, but it did not fit in this place, in these confused streets. He was humming the words of a song; Angelo couldn't tell which.

His voice was crude. But the sound still tore a hole of sadness in Angelo's heart.

Angelo passed him, crossing through the security gate and turning out of the block and into one of the busier intersections in the neighborhood. As he was about to cross the street, a white van came screeching round a corner, bounced off the sidewalk and hobbled back onto the road. Angelo had only a second to make a dive for the other side of the road. He heard the van roar behind him, and the driver honked his horn.

Angelo barely saw the van's rear end as it disappeared in another street.

He muttered profanities, rising to his feet again. He patted some dirt off his jeans and checked for any scratches. His elbows and forearms had a few, but nothing too serious. *That could have ended differently*, he thought. The man was inches from hitting him.

He pushed the thought away, thinking again of Kimberly. He had to figure out a way to end this. Well, maybe not to end it entirely, but at least to snap Kim out of her trance. Whatever it was that was keeping her that way, it was something chemical. Nothing else. It wasn't 'she' herself that was different, that was saying—doing —those horrid things, it was some chemical imbalance in her brain. At least, that's what the man on the news suggested. It made sense, though. More than— what? Some entity in the sky? Something winning her love, her affection? No, that didn't make sense. Chemicals made sense. That was something Angelo could wrap his head around.

He began walking again, this time cautious of any dangers lurking at the corners of the street. He arrived at a neighborhood called "Golden Heights." He'd seen the area a million times while driving to work, but since he didn't know anyone who lived there, he'd never given the place a second glance. Now, on foot, he noticed how proper and well-maintained the place looked. At least, in comparison to his own neighborhood. The houses were larger too. He walked up to the guard gate. This one, unlike the rinky-dink fence guarding his community, was enormous and sturdy; the gate was almost taller than his house and thick with a tangle of elegant yet impenetrable bars.

The guardhouse, however, was empty. *I guess this guy called out of work too*, he thought. *Or maybe it's a woman, and she's out in her uniform making a scene at home . . . just like Kim.*

Angelo shook his head. "No," he mumbled.

He stepped into the small guardhouse and gazed momentarily on the empty rolling chair before turning toward the controls. There was a small television set plopped in the corner against the glass. He tried a few buttons on the large panel before pressing one near the door. As soon as he pressed it, he heard the scratchy sounds of the gate opening, then an eerie, long screech as it opened completely.

He looked around nervously before stepping in. He wasn't quite sure why he was there, instead of back home helping Kim. He just wanted to see what was going on elsewhere; to get more information on how he could help his wife.

He heard a scream. It was a woman's voice.

"Stop it!" she yelled. She sounded at least a block away.

Angelo couldn't help himself as he began sprinting towards the noise. He was surprised at how much energy he had bottled in him as he stopped behind an old blue sedan.

"Say it one more time . . ." a man said in a pitchy voice.

"No," the woman said. She was probably in her early fifties, if Angelo had to guess.

"Good," the man said.

"I know he'll save me—"

"Who!" the man shouted, the scratchy blast of his voice sounding through the open air. "Who will save you?"

The woman, who had nest-like hair and droopy eyes, spat in the man's face. He slapped her hard across the face even before wiping the spit off. The slap connected hard and rang in the air before dissolving.

He felt a rise of anger sprout in his chest. All the anger that needed to be released. Because otherwise, he thought he might kill himself. Before he could think twice, Angelo was tossing the man against the ground. He punched him, feeling the man's nose crack, and seeing blood run down his lips. The sight only made Angelo more angry. He hit him again. Repeatedly, losing himself in this drug of rage. When he finally stopped he could hear the man moaning, his eyes closed. His face was mostly bloody, and Angelo felt a burning pain in his knuckles. He'd never been in a fight in his entire life.

Behind him, he heard something. It sounded like "thank you."

With his adrenaline still in full gear, he turned to see the woman smiling at him. The woman who was probably the man's wife. And she'd thanked him.

◀

IT TOOK A WHILE for Angelo's blood to cool. When it did, he moved along to the next block. This block was more crowded, and even before he saw the women in the streets he heard their avid praises. One elderly woman in particular caught his attention. She looked to be about eighty, and she was wearing a cardigan sweater and had her white hair pulled back in a tight bun. She was in a rocking chair, her lips overlapping themselves in a flabby line. Even from a distance Angelo could see the glimmer of tears in her eyes. But all this wasn't what had caught his attention about the woman.

It was the old man sitting beside her who had caught his eye. It was a loveseat rocking chair, fit for two people. The man had a look of nullified hope in his eyes, and he was slouched slightly, looking sadly at the hem of her long skirt. He was saying something, but Angelo couldn't hear. Angelo walked closer along the fence and tuned his ear to the man's voice. When he was close enough, he heard what the man had been repeating over and over. Angelo shuddered as he passed him by, pretending not to hear him. But Angelo could hear him clearly. The old man probably knew that Angelo was listening, but it was clear he didn't care even if the whole world was listening.

"Fifty-eight," the old man was mumbling over and over. "Did they mean a thing? Fifty-eight. My angel, did they mean a thing? Fifty-eight years together?"

◖ SEVEN

HE KNEW WHAT HE HAD TO DO. Not how, not even when, but somehow seeing that old couple, and seeing that old man nursing his sick wife, snapped some sense back into him. And he knew that he could never leave Kim's side again. She was his wife. *His* wife. She had to still be redeemable. She just had to be.

He'd failed her in the past. He knew that and he wasn't proud of it. But this was a fresh start for them. Granted, he wasn't sure if she would remember him taking her captive in the bedroom, interrogating her, but that was something he couldn't control.

He was back home now, watching her again from the window. The sun was below the trees and the houses, but its brilliance still spilled orange light over the sky like a wet drape. Maybe it was his imagination, but he felt as if he could physically see Kimberly's loss of weight, even from inside the house. Her clothes looked just a little more ill-fitted, like a limp flag on a pole, without wind to give it life.

Think, dammit, he thought irritably, pacing the floor of his small kitchen, his eyes rhythmically retracting from and coming into view of his wife. *Romance. Flowers. Courtship. Love. Love. Shit.*

He thought about the old man and his wife again. The way the man had accessed the situation (though probably without knowing so); he was just . . . loving her. Perhaps in the only way he knew how. And had Angelo seen something in her eyes? The faintest glimmer of recollection? Maybe not; maybe that was just dumb hoping on his part, or a response to the sky and not the old man, but he wanted to believe that what he'd seen had been a better solution than interrogating and shaking love out of his wife's shoulders. A better response than beating his wife to submission like he'd seen the other man trying to do. *So what, then?* he wondered. Was he to sit outside with his wife, weeping and wailing until she came to her senses? She may never flinch from the spell, so was it worth the pain of seeing her that way again? He had to believe that it was. Or maybe he had to believe that this drug would wear off after some time and everyone would be back to normal. Why not? Doctors were probably working on a cure right now. Male doctors. The thought racked through him. He shivered.

"I'll go out," he said, standing by the door.

The day was waning away, the sky shoving the sun beneath the world like a bullying older brother. Kim was sitting now, her eyes fixed on the woman across the street. The one who had the gun. The woman was standing, but Angelo didn't see the gun. He feared for Kim's safety.

"Hey," he said from behind her.

She turned and glared at him, regarding him as a disgusting rodent. "What do you want?" she said.

Angelo swallowed. *I guess she does remember*, he thought.

"I just wanted to see if you wanted any food? I can make you something," he said.

She looked away. First, to the woman across from her, then to the darkening sky. "My fasting is a testament to my love."

"You shouldn't have to suffer needlessly for love," he said.

She scoffed. "Nothing done in love is ever needless. You're some expert," she said sarcastically.

"Well, I love someone too. So I do know the feeling."

"Not like this, you don't." The way she said it made him shiver. But the temperature outside seemed to be dropping as well.

He wanted to shout at her, What you're feeling isn't love, sweetheart! It's a little thing us Realists like to call obsession!

But he didn't say it. Couldn't, because he knew that that approach was folly. He was here because he wanted to try a different approach, and that was to love her in the very most basic way. He had to be genuine about it if he hoped to get through to her.

The answer came to him suddenly. Perhaps the only way to win her back was to be equally obsessed about her. He didn't know exactly what that entailed, but it was a start.

But the answer remained incomplete—what was the best way to love her, in this insane situation?

She was looking across again at the woman. They seemed to be looking at each other. Angelo could see his wife's chest rise in angry spurts, then deflate. The woman across seemed too calm for comfort. And again, Angelo thought about the gun she had earlier.

"Who is she?" Angelo asked. He really didn't know, which was sad because that couple had lived across from them for at least five years.

Kimberly injected poison into her words. "Just another bitch trying to steal my Love," she hissed.

Angelo couldn't help wincing at her words again. He saw the woman across twitch angrily, and he was sure that she'd heard Kim say it.

"He's mine, you whore," the woman said, her hands balled in bloodless fists. "You'll know when this is all over."

Kimberly seemed to be steaming with anger now, and Angelo feared that she would suddenly run off to attack the woman, and that she would rear up her hidden gun and shoot Kim.

He couldn't let that happen. And then it dawned on him. This was how he would love her. This was the way to prove that, despite Kim's complete betrayal, he still would do anything to see to her happiness. He remembered then: the woman had thanked him and smiled.

Yes.

Yes.

Yes. Something holding his sanity was cut loose at that moment, and before he could stop himself, he was running to attack the woman himself.

❨

SHE TURNED SHARPLY to repel him, but he was already on her, shoving her hard to the asphalt. A few feet away from them, flies were swarming over her dead husband's carcass. She made impact with the ground, her head thumping against cement, and screamed. Angelo didn't know what he had planned on doing; he only knew that he wanted Kimberly to watch. And she was doing so with wide eyes.

"You son-of-a-bitch!" the woman roared. "You're gonna pay!"

Before Angelo could stop himself, he threw an open hand across her face, and the sound of the hard slap shot through the air. She screamed again, writhing like a possessed beast. Then she pulled something from somewhere beneath her thin clothes.

It was the gun.

One shot was released, but it missed terribly to the side. Angelo was too strong for her, even with her inspired rage. He slammed her hand—the one that held the gun loosely—against the cement until she was forced to let it go. Then he shifted over to grab it quickly. The woman spat in his face. Angelo spat back onto hers.

Then he looked over at his wife, who was gawking at the whole scene with disbelief. But at the same time, with a sense of excitement and approval. Like she was enjoying the show.

"Let go of me, you pig!" the woman was screaming. But Angelo had already tuned her out. It was his wife he needed back. And he was going to get her back, no matter what it took.

What happened next was something that humans had done since the dawn of mankind. But when it happened, just as it was about to happen now with Angelo, it always came as a surprise. Because even the darkest hearts must look inwardly at themselves in that moment. In that moment, they must break themselves down to something less. Something much less than what they were.

He felt his heart explode in hot panic. What was he thinking? What was he really considering? He heard a thousand voices yelling at him to stop. Telling him the

obvious, the thing that any moral person knows—
Murder is wrong! Murder is wrong! Murder is evil!

But I have to play her game, another infinitesimal voice whispered, even as he was shaking uncontrollably over the twisting woman—even as he raised her gun in his hand and cocked it.

Nothing done in love is ever needless, his wife had said. And he knew she was watching now, probably with terrifying glee.

He aimed the gun just above the woman's nose and pulled the trigger.

◖ EIGHT

THE PROGRESSION OF THOUGHTS that bubbled in Angelo's mind after the shot rang out were sporadic and over-whelming. It was a mesh of screaming voices, each one sounding more terrified than the last. It was a never-ending stream of words; haphazard, often incoherent. He pushed himself off the dead woman and her body shook slightly, a pool of blood drawing itself like a sick pillow beneath her head. Sooner than he expected, before even checking on his wife, Angelo turned and erupted a pumping stream of warm vomit on the ground. It landed like old soup and, feeling dizziness swell in him, Angelo almost dunked his hand into the puddle. He fidgeted and turned to Kimberly in a fog of disbelief. She stared at him blankly. The moon had over-taken the sun's heavenly throne.

"Kim—" he said breathlessly, taking sight of his shirt and arms that were splattered with blood and sweat.

Her mouth was agape.

"I did it—" he said, feeling his stomach flex in swishing contractions, making him want to throw up again. "I—I—"

He make an awkward gesture that landed him on the ground, and he sat up on his knees. Then he started to tremble profusely and weep. "Oh *my God!*" he screeched, slapping his shaky, bloody hands on the cement ground. He was sobbing like a child. What had he done? He'd really killed that woman. Then a voice, trying to still his chaotic thoughts, swept in: *But she killed her husband*, it offered. *She deserved it.*

No, no, he couldn't believe that. But it didn't matter. It was done and that was that. He looked up at Kimberly. Her eyes were wide like open wounds, studying him.

"Thank you," she said finally, in a still, cool voice.

Angelo looked down. "It isn't enough, is it?"

"Enough—?"

"You still love him," he said.

She was silent a moment. "Yes, of course. That will never change."

"Right," Angelo said, rising on his trembling legs. "Get in the car."

"I will not—!"

"Get in," he said levelly. "I'm not finished yet."

She stared at him with tired hesitation. "Finished?" she said.

He was already opening the car's passenger door for her. "Do you want to win this thing or not?" he said.

"SEATBELT," HE SAID, and she twitched to action and buckled herself in. Before he backed up the car, he turned to look at her. She looked utterly afraid, as if she was in the car with a complete stranger. It made Angelo want to sulk, but he was already getting used to the feeling. In the closed space of the car, he could smell sharply, from his clothes and skin, the scent of blood and brain matter. It made him want to retch again, so he blasted the air to its highest setting. It came gusting to life.

"I feel like I'm in a dream," he muttered. Kim looked away and said nothing.

"Look at me," he said. She did. "What do I have to do? What do I need to do to help you? Do I need to—" he broke off, feeling the electric urge to pound his fists against the steering wheel or the dashboard. He suppressed it. "Do I need to kill every woman in the block for you? In the neighborhood? The world?"

She stared at him in baffled suspension.

"Well?" Angelo probed, louder than he meant to.

"I'm his," she mumbled.

"Yeah, yeah—" Angelo said. "I just killed that woman for you. *For you.*"

"And I said thank you," Kim pressed.

"Do you realize what murder is? Murder?"

"I do." Her casual tone chilled him.

He reared his head against the leather headrest and sighed. The car sat idly, its engine humming softly like a bored child. He couldn't imagine killing someone else. It would change everything. It would haunt him for the rest of his life (more than he already felt haunted). Was all this worth it? Was Kim worth it? He felt embittered to think it, but they were questions he needed to answer if he was to make a wise decision.

Wise, a voice bickered. *Wisdom has no place here—not if you want to win her back.* But what if the drug wears off? He'd be killing needlessly. Killing, goddamit! He was shivering endlessly, feeling his breath escape him with every intake, as if inhaling only exhausted more air from his lungs.

"I need to know more about this—" Angelo said tiredly. "Is there anything else you can tell me?" He felt on the verge of tears.

From the corner of his eye, he saw Kimberly slouch in her chair. "You brought me into the car because you promised to help me. If you're not, then I'm leaving." She started to reach for the door handle, but was forced back when Angelo wheeled the car out of the parking space in reverse. The car jerked and squealed, and in an instant they were streaming through the street. Angelo's heart seemed to be throbbing more violently than the car was accelerating, and he briefly wondered how on earth he hadn't fainted or had a heart attack yet. The streets were crowded with at least twenty women and an almost equal number of husbands or sons or brothers. *This is it, right here*, Angelo thought. *The world, myself included, will die tonight. But Kim will love me in the end.*

He whipped the car to the left, towards the standing, dancing, fighting, shouting hoards of humans. Crazy, yes, but otherwise innocent humans. He didn't let himself think that as the front of his car collided into the first of the bodies at about fifty miles per hour. The noise of their skin-packed bones hitting the car and windshield was a sound Angelo had never thought he'd hear before. And they screamed. The women, the men, young and old. He hit nearly the whole row of them—at least, the ones who hadn't expected him in time to jump out of the way (and there were few of those). It grew silent in the car at the end of the block, and just then did Angelo realize that he had been screaming the entire time. Tears welled in his eyes without control. He heard the sounds of screams from outside, even with the windows up. Which meant only one thing—the job wasn't finished. Kim stared at him in disbelief as he veered the car in a tight semi-circle and ran them over again.

And again.

◀ NINE

IT WAS A MASSACRE. There were a few he didn't kill; some because he couldn't make contact and some because—despite his best efforts—he couldn't bring himself to. They had either ducked away behind cars or ran away. The men who were still alive were crying for their dead loved ones, and probably waiting to kill the driver behind the wheel of the car. Angelo didn't know what to do next. He drove the car through another block, away from the one he'd just passed. Away from the graveyard of corpses that now littered the streets.

Oh my God. The reality of the situation hit him like club blows. He was a lunatic. He was the mass murderer you heard about on the news, the psycho killer. It was him. He couldn't even throw up. He couldn't cry anymore. He didn't deserve that release, that luxury. He deserved to be as cold as a stone. That was, after all, all that psycho killers felt, wasn't it?

Kimberly said: "You really did it."

It brought him back and he looked at her numbly. He only nodded.

"Good," she said, but this time she sounded more hesitant, as if she too was aware that she was riding shotgun alongside a psychopath.

"And now?" he said, surprising himself with the ability to speak.

"Now I'm that much closer. And those bitches will never get in my way again."

Angelo nodded again. Gripped the wheel. *So I keep going,* he thought, feeling another band of sanity snap inside himself. He was no longer who he thought he was all these years, and he no longer lived in the reality he thought he knew. He spun the car into the next block and stopped before another row of people outside. It was dark outside, but the lamplights overhead and the headlights of his car allowed most of them to be seen. This group was more scattered, but their behavior was the same—shouting, dancing, fighting, and some weeping with joy.

"I want those smiles gone," Kim said beside him.

He winced. Then he smacked his foot onto the accelerator. The tires scratched the road like a mad feline. Thirty—forty miles per hour—but after he had hit two people (a woman in her late-forties and what looked like her husband) the car lost control and spun until it crashed into a parked truck. Angelo and Kim were wagged around like plush dolls beneath their seatbelts.

When everything was still, Angelo turned to Kim. "Are you okay?" he shouted.

"Fine, fine!" she said. "Get me out of this death trap."

They unhooked their belts and Angelo helped her out of the car. The whole front of the car was made into crumbled paper. The window on Angelo's side was smashed in, thousands of glass chips sprinkled on the seat of the car and on the ground outside. They didn't have much time to brush the glass and debris off their clothes, though, because about fifteen of the surviving men and women that had escaped the wrath of Angelo's car were running at them now, about a block away. Some with weapons.

◖

LUCKILY, IT WAS NIGHT. They were two blurry shadows as they shuffled behind the rear of the truck, crouching.

"Run! Run, Kim!" Angelo ordered in a loud whisper, tugging her arm. She responded frantically. They both ran as the screams behind them grew more furious.

"There they are!" a man shouted not too far off. And now the rest of the neighbors from the block, who previously thought that the car accident was a mere accident, were shifting their faces to anger as well. They were surrounded. They would have to use the darkness to their advantage. From where he was, Angelo saw two viable options: they could either try jumping over the fence of the nearest house, and try breaking in; or they could try to stealthily walk in between the crowd of people who hadn't noticed them yet, blending in, and come out the other side unscathed before the mob found them. Angelo decided on the latter option, since the fence would cause too much attention and only hide them for so long. Plus, he already knew that Kim was a terrible climber. And he had to keep her safe. She was the priority; worth killing for.

Each time he thought of the word, it sent a brand new echo of torment to his stomach and chest, making him feel light-headed and nauseous.

"Follow me and keep quiet," he whispered, leading her by the hand.

They moved quickly into the crowd on the far side of the street. Most of them were women, and most were oblivious to what was going on, their heads outstretched to the black expanse above them.

But the mob was moving fast; less than a block away now. "C'mon, c'mon—hurry!" Angelo whispered, running and jerking her arm. She kept looking back and up and every way but ahead of her. They were in the thick of the crowd now, maybe not completely veiled, but it was the best Angelo could hope for.

"There he is!" a man shouted from the front of the mob. The others hollered in response, sprinting faster and gripping their weapons tighter.

"Shit," Angelo muttered, out of breath. He needed to distract them. He needed to divert their attention somehow. His head swung so swiftly and heavily that he thought his neck might snap. *Use your surroundings*, he thought desperately. But there was nothing around him now except more stunned women, gazing upwards.

That's it.

"Hey!" he shouted, letting go of Kim's arm and grabbing another young woman. She must have been only seventeen years old at most. She was pretty with blonde hair. She must have been quite a catch in her high school. But out here she was only bait. The girl squirmed at his violent grip and screamed. But Angelo wouldn't let go. He had killed many people already. His mind was already set on killing anyone who got in his way, because he needed to protect Kim. He muttered an apology to the girl.

"This girl," he said shoving the young frightened girl to the ground, in the middle of the crowd, "is trying to steal your Love from you! Kill her!"

Angelo didn't quite know what he expected. But he didn't expect what happened. At least not the way it did. The women—all whom had had their heads directed to the sky in an awkward position—suddenly darted their heads and eyes to the girl on the ground. A scream broke from their mouths. The most horrible sound Angelo had ever heard in his life. As if the women had all just experienced the most ripping, carnal pain in their lives. Their fingers twisted in their uprising hands like talons, and they were on her even before Angelo had time to point at the girl on the ground. The girl who was now crying, terrified as the first of the women leaped onto her fragile young body. Angelo felt a shudder of guilt pulse in him, almost worse than when he'd killed the others. Maybe because she was so young. So pretty. He forced the thought away and turned to get Kim again. But she, like the others, was running to attack the girl.

"No, Kim!" he shouted, pushing through the crowd. He found Kim and grabbed her. "I tricked them, come on!" he screamed in her ear. She looked at him and nodded. But before he turned away completely, he caught a glimpse of the young blonde girl. Or what was left of her. Her face was a wet, red bowl of blood. Like a soggy bread bowl. She was naked, her breasts settled flatly against her chest, consumed with deep scratches about half an inch thick.

Angelo turned away and ran with Kim. Angelo felt like dying. He wanted to turn himself in for all his evils and fold over and die. But he couldn't while Kim was alive.

His plan had worked. The mob got lost in the crowd. And soon, everyone lost in that crowd broke into a deadly fight. Screams and cries and fists broke in the night sky as Angelo and Kim ran further away, turning into the next block. And that's when Angelo saw it.

Felix's burned down house.

"Hey! Angelo? That you?" he heard Felix say from the window of another house next to his burned one. "Get your ass in here! It's a fuckin' war zone out there." He waved a rifle through the window. "I got your back, bud."

Angelo sighed relief and ran with Kim to the front of the house. He'd finally found a thin stream of hope. And in such an unlikely place. There was no way he could know that the hardest was yet to come.

◀ TEN

THE HOUSE WAS a two-floor villa with a tidy kitchen, a small living room with a big TV and one bedroom downstairs, two upstairs. Felix explained that he had raided the house after his burned down. His sister, Valerie, was in the house now as well. She was a chunky girl, and short like her brother. She had a pretty face, but that face was puffed with swelling fat that hung off her chin like a plastic bag filled with water. She was tan, also like Felix. He hadn't explained in detail how he'd been able to stabilize his sister and convince her to stay inside the house, but Angelo guessed that, like himself, Felix had some demons of his own; things that he did to convince his sister that he was on her side. Of course, that was only a guess. In truth, Felix seemed like a passive guy. Angelo used to consider himself passive, as well, though.

They were all four sitting in the living room, sipping on mugs of coffee. Angelo was grateful for that, since his energy felt completely depleted.

"So," Felix said. "Why were you two running?"

Angelo tightened his lips, then leaned in to fetch the mug on the coffee table. He looked at Kim to stop her from saying anything about the killing, and hoped that she understood what his eyes were saying. Then he looked at Felix. "A fight broke out," he said. "All the women were attacking each other and we had to rush out."

Felix nodded. "I hear that. Seems like things are getting crazier out there by the hour. I saw some asshole driving a car through the street not too long ago, just pummeling over people. Can you believe that? I mean, what the fuck."

Angelo felt his face flush, and his hands went numb. The fact that he didn't drop his mug was nothing short of miraculous.

"Things are getting worse," Angelo offered.

Felix sighed. "Fuckin' right."

Angelo noticed the whole time that Valerie was staring at Kim, and she was staring right back. It made the room grow thick with discomfort. Angelo tapped a finger against his knees.

"No liquor?" Angelo asked finally.

Felix shook his head. "Not a drop. And believe me, I checked thoroughly. These people musta been religious or something. Well damn. They're probably meeting their Maker as we speak."

Angelo shifted uncomfortably in his seat. He almost draped an arm over Kim's shoulders—force of habit—but quickly retrieved it. He didn't need to backslide after everything he'd done to bring her this far. Though it could be debated, he thought he could sense a bit of change in the way she was treating him. Granted, this change was minuscule, probably imperceptible to anyone but him, but he felt it like the first hint of Spring. It made him feel easy, if only for a moment.

They spent the night there. Kim and Valerie insisted on staying outside, so the men didn't have a choice but to let them. They agreed on sleeping in shifts in order to keep an eye on the girls. Felix offered to take the first shift. And though Angelo felt possessive of Kim and didn't want her out of his sight for a second, he was too tired to debate. He slept downstairs where, through the window of his room, he could still at least see Kim and the others. Felix was sitting on an old wicker chair near the door, and Angelo could see him scratching his balding head from time to time. Kim and Valerie were standing only a few feet apart, constantly looking from the sky to each other. Kim had her arms crossed.

He watched them for about ten minutes before drowsiness weighed him down and he couldn't keep his eyelids open. The mattress slid under him like a seductive woman. The pillow kissed his warm, tired cheek and the blankets wrapped over him like sensual embraces. In a second, he was asleep. He slept for a satisfying three hours before Felix nudged him in the dark.

"Hey," he whispered. "Man, get up. Switch up."

Angelo stirred awake. He flinched when he saw Felix standing over him. He was rocking sleepily.

"I can't stay up another minute, man," he said. "You gotta cover me."

Angelo nodded, sitting up in bed. "Of course."

Now Angelo was outside sitting in the wicker chair, and he wondered if Felix was peering through the window at him. Unlikely, because the man had been so tired. He watched Kim. And Valerie. They were both standing. How could they not be tired? How could they not want to sit down after all this time? These were questions added to the cabinets of questions Angelo had, all which still floated in the hallways of his mind unanswered.

The incipient minutes seemed to crank through time with the sluggishness of a snail. He felt more awake than before, but not enough so to shake off the sense of lethargy in his bones. Making him start, Kim suddenly came over to him.

He sat up straighter.

"Hey," she whispered. "You got a second?"

Angelo nodded, fumbling his hands over his thighs. He hadn't felt this nervous around Kim since they began dating seven years ago.

Kim sat on her knees beside the wicker chair. This was the first time since the event that Kim showed any sign of normality. The fact that she was coming to talk to him was a titanic step of progress, something to be celebrated.

"I wanted to thank you again," she said. "For helping me this whole time."

Angelo caught his breath. He was almost beginning to feel that he'd been doing all of this more for himself than anyone else. To say he tried his best. He had believed at the time (though now he was beginning to doubt it) that he would sleep better knowing he'd killed those innocent people than if he were to give up on Kim. He wanted to know that he tried. That he did everything he could. But he hadn't really expected it to work. In fact, he didn't quite know what he was expecting. But now, it seemed that all this wasn't in vain after all.

He smiled wantonly. "I'm doing it because I love you," he said. "Do you understand? I love you the same way you love—him." He felt his hands trembling as he spoke. He felt like a high-schooler confessing his affection to a crush. But this was his wife. Will he ever again be able to treat her as such?

She spoke lower than before, almost inaudibly, and moved her lips closer to his ear.

"I—" she started, her eyes wavering around like floating bees. "I understand—but—"

"Yes?" Angelo said, leaning in closer as well. Their skin was almost touching.

"I need one more favor from you."

Angelo felt depleted. He nodded like a stiff bobble head. "Which is?"

She swallowed, then placed a hand on his lap. The touch sent a ripple up his legs.

"I need you to help me take care of—" She motioned to Valerie, who was standing a few feet behind them. "Her."

This favor, unlike killing those people in the street, meant something else. This was someone he knew. The sister of—a friend. Felix had been good to them. He'd allowed them to stay at his hideout without questioning them or treating them differently. And if it were the other way around, Angelo knew that he wouldn't do the same for him and his sister. Angelo was too careful, too defensive.

But it could mean a big step in the right direction for them. Kimberly was changing. She was responding now. He knew it. He felt it. *It's just one more person*, he thought, as if that would make the sin less vile. But no, even he knew that wasn't true. If he killed Valerie, he would have to kill Felix as well. The only person in the neighborhood he trusted. And someone he very much knew didn't deserve to die. The people outside were violent. Though it wasn't really true, that was something he could cling to when the guilt surfaced—as it surely did at least once every waking minute. But Felix—he wouldn't hurt a fly. Angelo could sense this about the man, and it made this task infinitely harder to commit to.

But—it had to be done. He was so close. So close to having his wife back. He figured that once she realized there was nothing up there in the sky, no prize to redeem for their efforts, maybe her love could be redirected back at him. It was a shot in the dark, but it was the only choice other than giving up on her. And that, he would not do.

So he came up with a plan the next morning at breakfast. The four of them were eating cereal on the counter that connected with the kitchen. There were only three stools, and Felix had offered to stand and eat in the kitchen. The offer only made Angelo feel more enraged and guilty because it was another sticker of proof that Felix was a good man and didn't deserve what he had coming to him.

"I—I got it," Angelo countered, and jerkily weaved his awkward body into the kitchen. Standing there, while the others sat and ate quietly, he'd considered his plan and spent endless minutes nit-picking at flaws and issues that would make it more difficult to do. Of course, these minutes weren't the sum of his planning and thinking; he'd spent the whole night planning and thinking, even when it was his turn to sleep.

He decided here in the kitchen—after much recycled thought—that using the gun to first kill Felix was the best option. Because if he died, Valerie likely wouldn't care. And that'll be much easier to deal with than if Felix were to find out that Angelo shot his sister. Angelo had hidden the gun in the drawer of the bedroom downstairs. The one where they'd slept. After breakfast, Kim and Valerie returned outside to watch the sky as was routine—they walked so slowly and awkwardly out of the house (because they kept exchanging angry glances at each other) that Angelo thought they'd never reach the lawn. When they did, Angelo closed the front door and walked into the bedroom. Felix was probably upstairs since he'd said he needed a shower. All that burnt debris from his house was in his skin, he'd said. And he couldn't rid himself of the awful smell. And that's where Angelo planned to do the job. He shivered fiercely at the thought of poor Felix in naked calm, probably enjoying the hot shower, only to see a shadowy figure silhouetted behind the plastic curtain like in Hitchcock's *Psycho*. And then seeing Angelo pull the curtain away and hearing the loud pop of the shot before the fatal bullet extinguished him from this world. It was an image that would haunt Angelo's mind forever, but it needed to be done.

He opened the drawer to retrieve the gun. But there was only Gideon's Bible sitting there in the empty cabinet.

"Looking for this?" Felix said from behind him, and Angelo heard the cocking of the gun.

◖

FELIX WAS HOLDING the gun up at him, but he hadn't pulled the trigger yet. But Angelo was waiting for it; it seemed that every muscle in his body—even the ones he didn't know were there—was in a hard flex. And his heart? He'd completely lost distinct feeling of it. Now it was as if his whole body was one uniformed unit, every part coated with surplus amounts of fear. When they faced each other, Felix's eyes were like what Angelo imagined the chamber of the gun to look like, housing small and deadly bullets, and his eyebrows pushed over his eyes like twin serpents.

"Felix," Angelo said, lifting his hands in surrender. He winced, because he almost expected to get shot down right then. But he wasn't.

"You know why I'm doing this, don't you?"

Angelo shook his head almost unnoticeably.

"I heard what your darling wife had to say about Valerie. I heard the whole thing last night."

Angelo feigned confusion. But he immediately knew. How could he be so stupid? To let Kim say those things right near the window? He wanted to punch himself for his idiocy.

"Don't give me that look. I'm sorry, but I want you both gone right now." Felix waved the gun toward the door with trembling hand. "Now, Angelo."

Angelo nodded, hands still in surrender, and he walked slowly to the front door. He didn't bother trying to explain; Felix was a smart guy, much smarter than he let on, and he knew Angelo's plan even at breakfast. Even when he offered to stand in the kitchen while they ate. It was all a trick. No, not a trick, a voice corrected him. He was looking for a reason to let you live. He was trying to help. Again.

Angelo walked out the door. The sun lodged beams of bright light against his eyes and he shaded it with his hands. Then he saw Kim. She was facing Valerie, and they were both breathing heavily. Their fists were closed.

"Kim, we're leaving," Angelo said, passing in between them.

Kimberly grunted. "Of course we're not. This bitch is leaving."

Valerie made an angry noise, but Felix was outside now and he shoved her back against the fence. "Don't try it!" he shouted at his sister.

Angelo turned to Kim in similar fashion and shook his head. "I have a plan, Kim," he whispered. "But we have to leave now. You trust me, don't you?"

She nodded quicker than he expected her too.

"Okay," he said. "Let's go."

They were gone before Felix had dragged his writhing, screaming sister into the house.

◀ ELEVEN

IT WAS ALL going to end soon, Angelo could feel it. The air outside was beginning to rot with the stench of corpses scattered in the street. They could see some of them— namely the poor bastards that had jumped into the crazy fight earlier—less than a block away. The ones who had survived (if any) were nowhere to be found. It was a ghost town; and Angelo thought if they were to rename the neighborhood right now, that might be the most suitable.

"So what now?" Kim said, noticeably out of breath. Her skin was coated with sweat and her hair hung pasted there on her glossy forehead. "What's this big plan of yours?"

Angelo had thought about it before, while looking at Felix's old house—a heap of burnt rubble and black debris. It was then, in the midst of the frenzy and thinking of a hundred things at once, that he got the one thought that shoved and shuffled and kicked its way past the others: *sacrifice.* That was the sum of real love.

And if the women were this obsessed, then they had to know it better than anyone else. And they had to know that the biggest sacrifice to make was in giving their own lives.

It was a sick thought that made Angelo question his very existence. But like a drowning man fighting a rampant current in the sea, he was too far in to turn back now. The only hope he had now was to let the current take him where it may. Be it insanity, malice, or even his death. He was on that ship from the beginning, and that ship set sail long ago.

They moved to another street in the neighborhood, this one even farther away from Angelo's home, but not so far from where Felix and Valerie were staying. As soon as they rounded a corner, they were faced with at least a dozen more women in the streets. The dosage of whatever drug they were on had to be increasing. Now, some of the women were rolling around the ground, scratching their bodies with the rough gravel, making themselves bleed. Some of the women had ripped off all of their clothing and were rolling around naked, scraping their breasts against the ground, and scratching and screaming madly. The fact that Kim wasn't partaking in this act was a testament to her improvement. She was being healed.

"My God," Angelo muttered, stepping slowly closer.

"What's the plan?" Kim said. "Do we run them over again? It'll be easier now that they're on the ground."

Angelo shuddered at the simple way they spoke of mass murder. "No," he said. "We crashed the car. And my plan is better. My plan will take care of Valerie and everyone else."

She grinned and pressed her hands together, mashing her palms together and letting out a low, sick chuckle. "Good," she said. "That's good."

They went back to their house first and got the materials he needed: chairs, tables, frames—any wood he could find. Then they got gasoline from their garage and the blow torch Angelo had used countless times on his car and others at the auto repair shop. He needed to start a big fire right in front of Felix's place—a fire that Felix wouldn't be alive to stop.

Kim helped him set the wood right at the front door of the house where Felix and Valerie were staying. It was exactly 6 p.m. when they'd finished breaking parts of the furniture and tossing it in a pile. Angelo had been listening closely to the sounds coming from the bathroom all day. The bathroom that was downstairs. You couldn't hear much, but a slight hiccup and hum came whenever the shower was turned on. He knew this because the walls were thin, just like the walls of his own house. When the time came and he heard the water turn on, Angelo would move in for the kill.

Angelo had to take care of Felix first. Realistically, he was the only enemy. The women were delusional and had nothing against him directly. So he would have to kill him in the shower, after all. He wasn't going to bother looking for the gun. He was a much bigger man than Felix, and if he caught him off guard, he could easily strangle him. *Strangle him*, echoed his mind. *Strangle him to death.* To death. Once he heard the shower come on, Angelo willed the thought away and moved around the fire to the sliding glass door at the back of the house. He smashed the window in with a piece of a chair. It made a sound louder than he expected and he winced. The glass fell like rain on the floor. No one was in this room. The lights were dimmed. He ran to the bathroom. Just as he reached it, the door opened hastily.

"What!" Felix screamed, a towel wrapped snug around his waist. "Jesus—"

Angelo grabbed his shoulders and flung him against the wall. The towel dropped, a wet heap on the ground. Angelo slipped on it and Felix punched him once across the face. Pain sprouted. He hit him again in the temple, and Angelo cried out, faltering against the sink. Angelo grabbed the acrylic toothbrush rack and slammed it over Felix's head. His head bobbled back, his eyes lolling briefly. Angelo took that moment to press his own body against him and push him back. Felix slipped on the wet tile ground and they both fell into the shower, Felix below Angelo. Felix's head collided with the bath spout on the way down and cut a small gash on his scalp. Blood began trickling out, but not enough to kill him. Felix regained some consciousness and began choking Angelo. The two men stared at each other intensely, their eyes the only living things in the room. Angelo felt the last of his air escape him, and just before he felt himself beginning to pass out, he flicked his eyes over to the right and saw a bar of soap. It was wet and looked almost new. He grabbed it quickly and used his other hand to pry Felix's mouth open. Felix bit down once but Angelo pried again. This time, Angelo's force was too strong.

Felix's mouth was agape as Angelo shoved the bar of soap into it. He could see the sudden fear in Felix's eyes. Poor Felix. Poor innocent Felix who wouldn't otherwise hurt a fly. The muscles above his eyes weakened as realization hit him. And with the slippery bar of soap in his mouth, it only took a gagging second before the bar was accidentally swallowed and lodged deep in his esophagus. He blinked a few times rapidly. Then he was still, and his hands lost their grip on Angelo's neck. Angelo could see the shape of the bar pressing the skin tight on Felix's neck like a glossy, pregnant belly.

◀ TWELVE

ANGELO FELT BETWEEN worlds as he moved to the front of the house. Kim was waiting for him there. He doused the pile with gasoline, then grabbed his torch and sprayed hellish fire upon the flammable wood. Immediately a loud whirl was heard and the world before them turned a bright orange, and a gust of hot breath shadowed over them.

The fire sizzled in front of them.

"What's this for?" Kim asked.

"I'm going to lie to them, Kim. But you have to understand that it's a lie. It doesn't matter what your heart tells you, it doesn't matter, okay?"

"What do you mean?" she said. "What's the lie?"

"I can't tell you yet. You'll know once this is all over. I just need you to trust me and go home, okay?"

"My home is out here with my Love."

For a second, Angelo thought she was talking about him, but then he remembered that she wasn't.

"You'll have your Love as soon as this is over. I promise. But you need to trust me, remember? You know that I love you, don't you?"

She looked away. "Yes, but I—"

"I know, I know," he said. "You don't love me back. But that's fine. Because love isn't about what you get out of it. Loving you is my choice. Even if I haven't been feeling it lately. I don't know what I'm feeling. But it must be closer to madness than love. But I'll prove I love you, Kim. I hope you see that. Everyone I've— everyone I've killed for you. I hope you see—" He looked away also, the fire dancing behind them. "We have to hurry. I don't know how much longer he'll be in there."

"But I want to watch them die," she said.

Angelo shook his head. "Kim, you can't. I'm sorry. You just have to trust me. You'll see why once this is over."

"Okay," she said hesitantly.

Then she ran home.

◖

BY THE TIME SHE WAS GONE, the fire was in full effect, blazing in the darkening night like a mystic beast. The house had begun to catch fire as well, and the whole time Angelo was circling the perimeter of the fire in a dazed stupor, feeling wholly disconnected with the world. Death was beginning to feel more like a glitch in a game than an actual tragedy. It was becoming easy, and that's what frightened him most. He expected Felix's death to affect him worse than all the others prior; but if he was honest, his death had probably been the easiest, if only because it had come last. As he reached a reasonable distance away from the fire, he wondered where Valerie was. Had she seen the fire, or heard the break-in or the fight? He gazed at the distant windows of the second floor and couldn't see anything behind them. Either way, she would die when the fire took up the whole house. But first, he had to lure in the other women.

He made his way back to the street where, surely enough, the same women lay writhing on the ground. Most of them naked, some of them well in the process. He walked along them, looking at them and feeling sorry for them. Wondering where their husbands were. Had they abandoned them? Had every man they'd ever known abandoned them? Perhaps the sky really was the only love they had now.

Angelo stood in the center of the block, wondering how he should begin. Instead of wondering, he just let instinct take over.

"You think that's love!" he bellowed, turning in slow circles so that all the women could see him. "You inflict scars on your body, you scream and writhe, but that's not enough, is it?"

One by one, the women began looking up at him. Their faces were sweaty, and dirt sat on that sweat like a muddy paste. Their eyes were forlorn, void of any humanity now; glazed over with an absentness of sheer lunacy.

"Of course it's not enough," he said, now that he had their attention.

"But what else can we do?" one woman said. "What else can we give him?" She was in her early-thirties, Angelo guessed, and wore a dirty white tank top and yoga pants.

Angelo had everyone's attention now. And now he had the power to send them all to their death. To give Kim what she wants and prove his love to her, and prove that her so-called love is nothing more than dumb obsession.

He lifted his hand to point at the fire less than a block away. The woman turned their gaze to it.

"You show him just how strong your love burns."

"Yes!" the women began to shout maniacally. "Yes! Yes! Of course!"

They began to each rise, each of them leaping to a sprint. They were shouting against each other, each of them pushing the other as they ran, and Angelo ran behind them. Even before he reached the house, he could see the fire blasting higher with rekindled intensity. The women didn't even flinch; or scream. They didn't make any sounds of pain. To Angelo, that was the most haunting thing about it. What drug could do that? One by one, the women sprung their bodies into the fire, all of them shouting only one thing as their bodies erupted into ghosts of fire.

"I love you! Look! See how I love you!"

Then, one by one, their bodies crumbled to the ground in quiet, burning piles.

◖

THE ODOR WAS too much to bear. Angelo fled from the street as quickly as he could, reaching his house soon after. He walked inside. As he passed the kitchen, he caught glance of the breakfast he'd tossed in the sink just a few days ago. The breakfast he'd made for Kim. That felt like a lifetime ago. Back then, he had thought that that was a sacrifice. Now he'd killed over thirty people in two days for her.

He searched the house; turning on the lights downstairs and upstairs, searching each room. But she was nowhere to be found.

"Oh no . . ." he said, feeling dizzy suddenly. She wouldn't. She wouldn't.

But of course she would.

Angelo ran out of his house, running in the blurry night past his street and back to the street where the fire burned boldly. The house was in flames as well now. Not completely, so there was still time.

He ran to the backyard, where the sliding glass door lay in shattered pieces like fallen snow. He stepped into the house. He could feel the hot air in the house as it slowly caught fire. He rushed upstairs. And as he was halfway up, he heard a gunshot that stopped him to a paralyzing halt. When the ringing in his ears mellowed, he returned to his senses and climbed the steps, faster this time. Then he saw her standing in the narrow hallway.

His Kim. And she was holding the gun. Her gown was matted with blood.

"Kim . . ." he said. She was a dark shadow in the even darker hall. Only the moonlight and the fire from outside glowed against her bloody gown.

She raised the gun at him.

"Kim, wait—please," he cried.

"I'm sorry," she said. "But I love him. And you love me. And I can't have you interfering anymore. He'll grow jealous, and then what?" Her hand trembled as she said the last part. And so did her voice.

"Kim, I helped you. Don't you see? I'm the one that loved you. I proved it to you. Why can't you . . . why can't you love me back?"

She remained silent.

Angelo felt hopeless. All the progress he'd made, everything he'd done to win her back, was for nothing. Nothing. He felt his body adrift, feeling split in multiple worlds, ethereal textures of life. What he was seeing was a multi-layered fabric before his eyes, cloths consisting of contradicting beliefs and hopes stitched with naivety. He never had Kim. This whole time. He'd never won her. She'd never made any real progress. She was playing him all along.

He suddenly didn't care about dying. In fact, he welcomed the idea. He just wanted a break from this whole venture. A break from his restless mind trapping him in dark corners of guilt and regret. Screaming at him that he's an evil man, a murderer, a liar. Shouting to him that he never knew a thing about love. No one did. It was either obsession with oneself or obsession with someone else, and there was no room for debating what was between the two.

Kim cocked the gun. "I don't want to kill you, Angelo. And I'm looking for any excuse not to. So I'm just going to let you leave. And I never want to see you again. Is that understood?"

He felt small in the room, a shrinking man being swallowed up by shadows and this woman he knew nothing about. Angelo's eyes began to brim with tears.

"Where's my wife?" he said, feeling his voice sound significantly smaller as well.

Kimberly stood steady now in the dark, her gun never wavering from his direction. "She's gone," she said.

This had to be the worst kill for Angelo. Worse than the first woman he'd murdered in cold blood with the gun. Worst than the dozens he'd run over like stray dogs, and the other dozens he'd sent to the fire. Worse than Felix. This was the death of all his hope. All his love. The prize he'd invested everything into—the death of his marriage.

"Where's my wife?" he said again, this time spitting the words and taking a bold step closer.

Kimberly didn't move, but her arm stirred hesitantly behind the gun.

"Stay back," she said. "Stay back. I'll shoot."

"Then shoot me," he shouted. He took another step closer.

"Back!" she cried. "Get back, dammit! Please, Angelo. Please."

He took another step. "No, Kim."

Her hand was trembling uncontrollably, and Angelo was waiting for her delicate finger to twitch on the trigger and send him wherever he'd sent Felix and the others. *No*, he thought. He didn't deserve even that mercy.

"I'm begging you," she wept.

"And I'm begging you," he cried back. "I've been evil to try to earn your love and I'm otherwise mad without you. I'm a murderer. I'm sick in the head, Kim. And I don't want to feel this anymore."

He was close enough now that he pressed his forehead against the barrel of the gun. It was still warm from the shot she'd used on Valerie.

"You're not evil," she said, almost choking on the words as tears fell like a stampede down her face. He thought he saw a sad smile drive by her lips. "You're good. But I—I can't," she said. "Don't you know that? I'm drowning in him. I'm wallowing. He's all there is!"

Angelo closed his eyes. Now he had to be dreaming. She'd called him good. There was no way she would say those words otherwise. The gun felt like a hot coin pressed against his forehead. It held there for a moment, then the pressure was released. He opened his eyes.

Kim had the gun pressed against her own temple. "I've done a greater wrong than you," she said. "Because while I swore to only love my One True—" she looked into his eyes. "I love you as well, Angelo."

Angelo thought he would drop to the ground then, feeling so depleted and exhausted. And now to hear this; it was too much for him.

She closed her eyes, and when Angelo thought she was going to really pull the trigger, he said everything he could to try to change her mind.

"Kim, he doesn't exist," he said. "If you love me, please listen to me now. He doesn't exist. He never did. It's only the sky, Kim. Only the sky. It—it was a drug, Kim. That's what the news said. It was a drug. We don't know where it came from. But it's not real."

Kim's eyes were pulsing and shaking in their sockets, filled with tears, seemingly considering everything he was saying. The gun scratched at her head with all her endless shaking.

"Not real?" she whispered. "A drug?" Her finger loosened on the trigger slightly.

It had happened. She was beginning to rid herself of all her drug-induced fantasies. He could see it in her eyes; they looked attentive again. Physically, they hadn't really changed, but the distant echo in them vanished away. She was looking at him again, as if for the first time.

"Angelo?" she whispered.

He smiled at her. His Kim. His wife. His love.

And that's when they heard it; a magnified voice that bellowed like speakers in a stadium. The ground rumbled with each syllable the voice spoke.

"ATTENTION. ATTENTION. ATTENTION. EARTH."

The voice came from the sky.

◖ THIRTEEN

KIMBERLY'S EYES WERE LOST AGAIN. Forlorn. And Angelo's last hope tailed behind them. She'd run downstairs, not caring about the fire that had begun to burn the kitchen and living room, blowing waves of black smoke like fatty bubbles. Thick fire covered half the room, and when Angelo went down there after her, he immediately lost himself in a torrent of bitter, lung-gripping smoke. He knew the fire was behind him and on his left; that's the only way he was able to find the exit at the back of the house—through the same broken glass door. There was still a great deal of smoke outside, and when Angelo couldn't hold his breath any longer, he released it and immediately fell prey to a coughing fit. It overtook him with impossible authority, and each time he tried to intake oxygen—which was practically every second—a blinding punch was traded for it. It was impossible to breathe, and he thought that he was going to die in the maze of smoke before he could reach Kim.

Eventually, though, he made his way out the side of the house, where the fire was absent. Soon it'd take over the entire house, though. He wouldn't be here when that time came.

He had to jump a fence to the neighbor's house, because the fire was too strong at the front of the house, where the burning bodies lay scattered like a grotesque constellation.

Once he reached the street, out of breath and energy, he saw Kimberly. She was, like she'd been before, staring up at the cloudy night sky with her arms outstretched.

And there was a beam of light shining a spotlight on her, piercing from out of the clouds. She and Angelo were the only living people in the street. The beam was dusty and dim, but it was definitely there. He even heard a low hum coming from that direction. Then she started to float upward. She was ascending. The humming grew louder, and Angelo began to cry out her name, running towards her. When he stepped under the light, it began to burn him, like he was inside a compact steam room. Terrified, he leaped out of the rim of light.

"Kim!" he cried again.

She was climbing the blank air slowly, as if her soul was attached to a winding fish line. She was thirty feet in the air now. Forty feet. Fifty.

Angelo was weeping, collected like trash on the floor, his tears seemingly gushing out of every pore in his body. What was happening? Was he dreaming? How could this be?

"Angelo!" she shouted through the infinite gulf between them. He looked up, barely able to view her through the screen of tears. He needed to hear it one last time. At least one more time. God, please, let her say it one last time. But she didn't say that she loved him. Instead, she began laughing hysterically. "I told you! *I told youu!*" she shouted joyfully, even as her tiny figure disappeared behind a cluster of lifeless clouds.

◀ EPILOGUE

THINGS WOULD NEVER be completely back to normal, but the world was trying its best to function as it did before The Courting—that's what the headlines called the event. Many questions still went unanswered about the event, and the world would never really know what happened in those three days, or where those 85 women were taken. That's exactly how many were reported "abducted." Kimberly included. In the entire population, only 85 women were taken. No one knew why that number. And in all the world, Kim had to be one of them. Of course, if Angelo hadn't helped her the way he had, she would have still been here on Earth. The drug wore off almost immediately after the final minutes of the abduction. All the surviving women became lucid again, not remembering anything that happened, and finding themselves in a world of chaos, with death all around them. Nobody was charged for their crimes in those three days. So Angelo, although he could still see their faces whenever he closed his eyes, was absolved of all his murders. The government couldn't arrest half the world for crimes they were influenced to commit. And though Angelo hadn't been drugged like the women, his actions were understandable given the circumstances. Other men around the world had committed similar crimes, either out of frustration and anger or by accident. There wasn't even a court hearing. Everyone just wanted to forget and move on, as impossible as that seemed. It took weeks for the streets to be cleaned up, for the bodies to be taken away and buried. 46 million people died in those three days. Considering the circumstance, that number seemed pretty low to Angelo. About 30 million of those people were female (young and old), the rest were male. About 15 million people were badly injured, and those who lived in America were taken care of free of charge, as if it mattered. A lot of those people didn't even want to be alive anymore—their mothers, wives, husbands, siblings stripped away from them. Many committed suicide. Had to be in the millions, if Angelo recalled correctly. He'd considered suicide, as well. But for some reason, he couldn't bring himself to do it. For some idiotic reason, he believed that maybe the aliens would bring his wife back some day. When they were finished doing whatever they were doing with her. It was idiotic, all right. Nobody knew what the aliens wanted those women for. People had their theories, though. The most popular theory was that the aliens wanted the strongest women they could find for breeding purposes. That made the most sense. Drug the women on Earth, get them to battle it out, and scoop up the winning bunch. Then put some prime male sperm in them and watch them make puppies for the aliens to play with. It sounded sick and outrageous, but it did make some sense. Another theory was that the aliens themselves were having sex with the women. Angelo didn't particularly like this theory, for obvious reasons.

So while he couldn't bring himself to put a bullet in his head, or treat himself to a gourmet dish of barred soap, Angelo did have the wisdom to admit himself into a mental ward (also free of charge) for a couple weeks. He thought maybe they could help him move on. They couldn't. No shock there. So Angelo returned home. His doctors allowed it, knowing themselves that they couldn't offer much real help. Even the doctors needed help. Everyone was affected the same. Everyone had lost someone that night.

◖

ANGELO COULDN'T SLEEP. He went downstairs to fill his glass with gin for the seventh time that evening. The bottle was almost empty. He reached the kitchen eventually, floating on blurry vision, watching the black shadows overlap each other as his eyes searched the room. He didn't want to turn on the lights, though. He liked the darkness, it let him forget that there was a world out there. The kitchen smelled awful; in three weeks he hadn't cleaned up the mess in the sink. The breakfast sat in a rotted heap, with dry vomit over it, and bugs would occasionally swarm the sink like immigrants, eating their fill and dancing around the old, fart and puke-smelling eggs and stale bacon and toast like they were celebrating some secret holiday. But he hadn't been able to bring himself to clean it out yet. He stood over the sink in the dark. The breakfast seemed to have a personality; sitting there like a kid afraid of his parents. There was a legion of ants roaming underneath the eggs. They wiggled around in the shadows like they were working the graveyard shift.

Angelo twisted on the faucet. The water ripped to life. The ants scattered about, fleeing the water storm. Most of them couldn't and were drowned instantly. It was, in a way, their own version of The Courting, and Angelo was the sinister being in the sky. He dumped the eggs, bacon, and toast in the trash can. Then washed the plates. The room almost immediately smelled better. He refilled his glass with gin, then went over to the window of the front door. The sun was showing its first signs of entry in the outlines of the clouds. He watched the sky pass by slowly, just like he did most nights, thinking about Kim and where she was. If she was even alive. If she was still in love with him, if the drug had worn off for her, or if she was still infatuated with whatever had been waiting for her up there. He took a sip of his gin and let the alcohol take him one step closer to forget-fulness. He knew it wouldn't last, though. When morning came, so with it would sorrow. He wondered if he would ever be able to forgive himself for what happened. Not just for the deaths, but for helping Kim. If he hadn't tried to love her, to win her back, she'd still be here and they would be in love. Instead, he'd fallen prey to the same drug she was induced with. Except his was self-induced.

In his little villa home, Angelo sipped gin and watched the parking space bumper where his wife had once stood, cursing, as he would the for the rest of his life, the sky that had taken her.

◖ Blind Date

THE *LUCKY LADY* was docked before him; a moderately grand charter yacht that advertised its quixotic and romantic presence even at first glance—maybe too much so. The words "The Lucky Lady" were stamped on the side in pink cursive. And if that wasn't vulgar enough, there were even little pink clovers sprinkled around the letters. It made Brian want to cringe. He shook his head and smiled. *Oh Emily,* he thought. *What mess have you gotten me into this time?*

A blind date—that was what. Christ, he was twenty-nine, not fifty. He didn't need a shove in the right direction when it came to women. Sure, he hadn't had a serious girlfriend since last April, when he'd dumped his ex, Nelly. But she was a troubled girl. *Clingy,* and to Brian, that was the worst breed of women. Brian knew that he was still a good man with plenty to offer a woman. Foremost in the area of money.

He reached the aluminum ramp of the boat and a man in a tuxedo greeted him there. *A tuxedo, how trite.* Brian had to grin. The man grinned politely back.

"Welcome aboard *The Lucky Lady,* sir. May I take your jacket?" He held his arms directly out as if he himself were taking on the form of a coat rack.

"That's fine," Brian said, smiling. Then he asked nonchalantly. "Has my date arrived?"

"Oh yes, sir," the man said, lowering his arms sheepishly. "She's waiting for you at the table inside."

He gestured his arm out to invite Brian in, and they stepped inside together. The dining room was compact, but with that little space they'd done a good job of adding texture to the room, and without making it seem gaudy or stuffy. The windows were tinted so that it hardly felt as if he were on a boat at all, and there was a thick walnut table draped with a crimson tablecloth in the center of the room.

Brian was escorted to a matching walnut chair and the tuxedo man nodded. "Wait here, sir."

He went away and Brian looked around. Where was his date? he wondered.

As soon as he picked up the menu and started eyeing through it, the boat came to life with a monstrous burp. He felt the ground vibrating beneath his feet like a giant cellular phone, and he imagined the boat drifting away from the dock.

But where's my date? he thought again.

"I'll call her," he mumbled to himself, reaching in his pockets for his phone. He dialed her number and waited. She picked up after only one ring.

"Hello?" his date answered anxiously.

"Hi, it's Brian," he said. "Heather? The boat's undocking. Where are you?"

"I know it is. I'm on the boat," she sounded frightfully excited. "Are you in here?"

"Yes, in the dining room."

"Where?"

"I said I'm in the dining room. Where are you?"

A slight pause. "I'm in here. Where?"

"Well it's not a big room. I don't see you."

Another pause. "Well, I'm here."

Brian shifted in his seat and grunted. "Are you on the right boat?"

She clucked her teeth. "The Lucky Lady?"

"Yes."

"*Yes,* I'm not dense."

"Is there another dining room?"

"Well, why would they seat us in two separate rooms?"

Brian shook his head and looked around the room again. He felt foolish, though, because the room was too small to miss another human being. For some reason, he found himself looking under the table.

He smiled. "Are you playing with me?"

"No," she said. "Are you?"

"I'm not."

"Are you in the restroom?"

"I'm not," he chuckled.

"Hmm."

"'Hmm' indeed," he said. "Will you come out now?"

He heard her laugh through the receiver. "I told you I'm *out.* I'm sitting on the far side of the room. The chair at the end."

"I'm near the door," Brian said.

"No," she giggled, "you're not."

"Hmm . . ." Brian said again. And there was an awkward silence that fell over the phone line.

"Prove it," he said after a moment.

"Pardon?"

"Prove you're here." He knew she couldn't, but for some reason he felt fear strike him in the chest.

"Okay," she said, annoyed. "A red table cloth."

Brian's heart twitched hollowly. "You're right. You guessed, though."

"Of course, I did. Now—how do *I* believe *you?*" she inquired. "You tell me something now."

"Okay." Brian looked around, the phone pressed tightly to his ear. "The windows are tinted. Oh—better—the menus are green and white. They have little clovers like the ones outside on the boat."

There was yet another silence. "This joke is getting old," she said playfully.

"I'm glad you think this is funny," he said, and he was sure that she could hear the smile behind his words, "because I'm very hungry and I'm not eating without you."

"Likewise," she said. "Oh—here comes the waiter now."

Brian turned, and the waiter—the same man in the tuxedo—was standing over him.

"Can I start you off with a drink?" he asked politely.

"Water, please," Brian said, and he almost laughed because he thought he sounded like a man dying of thirst in the desert.

"Right away, sir. Would you like to see our wine menu?"

Brian looked across the table again, to where his date claimed to be sitting.

"Can you find out for me if the lady wants a drink, first?" he asked. He didn't intend for it to sound like he was reprimanding the waiter, but when the neat man blinked nervously, shook his head and said, "Where are my manners?" Brian realized that it came out the wrong way.

He expected the man to ask about the lady's where-abouts, but instead, he walked over to the far side of the room. Brian felt the next beat of his heart send a ripple of frightful disbelief throughout his entire body. It wasn't possible for . . . no, not possible at all.

But the waiter said it, said the words that made Brian's face flush. Though he couldn't see his own face, he could almost feel the pigmentation of his skin wither away, fleeing his miserable face. Brian lowered the phone.

"Can I start you off with a light Moscato?" the waiter asked the empty chair, then nodded and smiled courtly. "Very well."

Brian shook his head in disbelief. The phone he held suddenly felt colder, as if the glass receiver were sucking away the comforting heat of his sanity.

The waiter began pouring the wine over the table, into the empty glass on the far side of Brian's seat. The

Moscato dribbled rhythmically into the thin glass, making a light sound like gargling diamond pebbles.

"Uh—" he stuttered, feeling sweat perspire from his hands. The waiter turned to leave. The wine glass sat filled, alone, like a deserted island.

"Jesus, did you see that?" he heard her say faintly through the receiver. "He was talking to thin air at the other end! What's going on?"

Brian couldn't speak. He watched the waiter leave the small dining room through the dreamy, fuzzy edge of his vision and swallowed dryly. Again, he couldn't speak. He wondered how she could.

"Hello?" she said after a moment. "Please don't hang up."

For an instant, Brian wanted to run away. He contemplated rising from his seat, probably knocking over the wooden chair, and fleeing the room; hurling the cursed cell phone at the tinted-mirrored wall.

But then his mind shifted. *Where would you go?* he thought remorsefully. *The ship has set sail.*

He made a sound with his throat that came without his consent. It sounded like a baby's burp.

"Jesus—hello?"

"What?" Brian snapped.

"Brian, *what is this?*" she pleaded.

"I don't know," he said.

The static between the lines was heavy, and he could hear her panicky breaths through the receiver.

Brian looked at the empty chair across from him again.

"You say you're really here," he said, and he wasn't sure if he meant it as a statement or a question. But he thought he meant it more as a question, because he wanted an answer.

"Are you?" he pressed.

"Jesus—*yes*, Brian. I swear I am," she said.

Brian nodded as if she could see him. "Okay, then. Well—what do we do?"

"What *can* we do?" she said, her tone softening.

Brian shook his head. "We can . . ."

"We can . . ." she mimicked.

"We can—eat. We can drink," he said.

She laughed. "And continue to lose our minds?"

"The waiter probably thinks we're nuts because we both have cell phones to our ears."

He heard her laugh. "I wonder if he saw us both."

"He must have," Brian said. "He took both our orders."

"Jesus, I can't believe it," she said. "What does it mean? How does that work?"

Brian grunted in thought. *What* did *it mean? How* did *it work?*

"Are you from another dimension?" she asked.

"Not that I know of," he said playfully.

"I think that must be it," she said.

"Oh but that's science fiction nonsense," he said.

"*Well*," she moaned. "Then what *is it?*"

"I don't know," he said. "But that—what you said—that can't be physically possible."

"Says who?"

He chuckled. "Says Logic, that's who. Says anything that's ever occurred in history. Who ever heard of two people being in the same room, but in different dimensions?"

She sighed. "Maybe it's this boat."

"That makes a little more sense," Brian said. "But it makes me uneasy all the same."

"Me too. Do you believe it, Brian?" she asked, sounding more serious, as if she still didn't quite believe it herself and wanted to see if he was foolish enough to.

Brian leaned back in his seat and glanced at the menu, then back up across to the empty chair.

"No, of course not," he said.

"Me either."

"Should we continue our date?"

"Our *blind* date?" she said.

Brian laughed, and so did she. He found himself tapping nervously at the red cloth of the table.

The waiter came back, walking hesitantly, obviously perplexed that the couple was still on their phones. They ordered their meals. Brian chose a rack of lamb with two side dishes of potato gratin and ratatouille. Heather ordered a simple fettuccini alfredo dish.

"Oh," Brian said, waving his index finger to the waiter. "And I'll have the best Merlot available."

"Right, sir." He nodded and went.

"How's the wine?" he asked, looking back to the chair.

"Mm—" she said, taking a sip. "Very nice, actually." The glass on her end, however, didn't move at all. *Of course it didn't*, he thought.

"So," he said. "What do you look like?"

He heard Heather cough a small laugh. "What do *I*? Hmm . . . would you believe me if I said I looked like a supermodel?"

Brian chuckled. "That would make this much easier to imagine."

"Okay," she said. "Really though—I have brown hair that reaches down my mid-back, green eyes, I guess a sort of thin face, high cheek bones . . . I'd like to think I'm not *too* far off from a model."

"Wow, humble too?" Brian mocked.

She giggled into the static. "I've got to come out on top here."

"Yeah, sure. My turn?" he asked.

"I already decided you look like Brad Pitt," she said. "Please don't ruin it for me."

Brian laughed again.

The waiter returned with their meals. He placed Heather's meal near the lonely Moscato, then came back to lower Brian's meal before him. Then he poured the Merlot. When the waiter was gone, Brian put his phone on the speaker setting and lowered it.

"Your food's going to get cold if you don't come in here," he said.

She was silent a moment. "Do you still think this is a trick?"

"I just can't believe the other possibility, so yes, I do."

"Well how do you think I feel?" she said irritably. "I'm in the same position as you."

"So what are we still doing here?" he said, feeling defensive for some reason. "Why don't we just up and leave?"

He could hear her breathing through the static. "You want to?" she asked.

He felt suddenly embittered. He still felt as if he was being fooled, as if Emily would pop out from the other room at any moment; laughing and pointing her finger, side by side with the waiter, who would be laughing too, because everyone was in on it. It was all some prank. Or a big magic trick. It had to be.

Surprising even himself, Brian rose sternly from the table. Heather must have heard the chair roll back, because she said quickly, "What are you doing?"

He didn't know whether he should be upset with her or not. Technically, she hadn't wronged him in any way. He just grunted. "I've got to go, I'm sorry."

He picked up his phone and turned off the speaker setting, then pressed the phone to his ear.

"You're really going?" She sounded truly disappointed.

"I've got to," he said.

When she didn't say anything else, he reached into his pocket and pulled out his wallet. From it, he slipped out a fifty-dollar bill and placed it on the table for tip. The meals were already paid for prior to his arrival.

"Are you still there?" he said.

"Yes," she said quietly.

"I'm sorry."

"Brian . . ."

"Yes?"

"I'm not tricking you. I'm really here. I wish you believed me."

He sighed heavily. "I wish I did, too. It was nice talking to you."

"It was nice talking to you, too," she said.

"I wish . . ." he started, then stopped at the door. "I don't know. I just wish I could see you. If you're not tricking me, that is."

"I'm not. And I wish so, too."

He sighed again and fingered the doorknob. "Well," he said. "I'm going to tell the captain to turn us back."

"Are you going to hang up?" she asked.

He couldn't explain why, but he suddenly felt the urge to run up to her and embrace her; to smell her hair, to feel her soft flesh pressed against his, to hear her friendly voice without the intruding sound of static—in other words, to experience her as a *woman,* and not as a distorted voice behind a cold cell phone. He gripped the phone tighter to snuff out his desire.

"I think that's best," he said.

She sighed and he could almost sense her shoulders slump. "Okay," she said after a moment. "Well . . ."

"Well," he said back. "It was an experience."

"It was a pleasure," she said. "But I guess," —she chuckled as she said this— "I guess it wasn't meant to be."

He offered a weak laugh. "That's life, huh."

"Yes," she said. "It's always something with me and men. Never works out. But I must say, parallel dimensions is a first."

He snorted. "Oh stop. We don't believe that." He unknowingly removed his hand from the doorknob.

She sighed again. "Of course not. It's . . ."

"Silly," he finished for her.

She sighed tiredly. "Yes. Very, very silly."

Brian switched the phone to his other ear. He then looked at the empty seat again. Now both seats were empty and both their meals were getting cold.

"Goodbye, Heather."

The static hummed, then: "Goodbye-bye, Brian."

He hung up the phone.

Feeling a draining emptiness in the pit of his stomach, Brian grabbed the doorknob aggressively. The door leaped open and he nearly bumped into the waiter. The waiter twitched, startled to see him.

"Ah," he said. "I was just coming to check on you, sir."

"Thanks," Brian said. "But actually, there's been a change of plans. We need to head back early."

The waiter's eyebrows perched up. "Oh?"

"Yes," he said. "Will that be an issue? I'm sorry for the inconvenience."

The waiter waved a hand and shook his head. "Not at all. I'll tell the captain right away."

He started to turn, and Brian spoke before he could stop himself. "Uh—one more thing," he added.

The waiter turned to him again, his face adopted curiosity. "Yes?"

"Have . . ." Brian started, then offered a small preparatory laugh. "This is going to sound silly, but have any of your former guests ever complained about . . . well, anything strange? On this yacht I mean."

When he saw the confused look on the waiter's face, he gave an embarrassed laugh and said, "I know, it's silly. I just—"

"Were you or the lady dissatisfied with the yacht?" the waiter asked. "Or the service?"

"No, no, it's not that." Brian shifted his weight uncomfortably and offered the smallest slice of a smile. "Forget I said anything. Please tell the captain as soon as you can."

The waiter nodded slowly. "Yes, of course." Then he turned and left.

Almost an hour later, the yacht had docked. Brian felt the rumbling of the boat lessen, like a monster being petted until it was fast asleep, until it was, for the most part, completely still.

He looked one last time to the table and the empty chair on the far side of the room. The chair where Heather had claimed to be sitting. He wondered if she was still there now, or if she had moved elsewhere in the small room. The thought made his skin crawl off. Maybe she was standing in his exact same spot, as if they were one person, within each other.

He scoffed gruffly. *Stop it, stupid man,* he told himself. *You're entertaining ridiculous notions. It was a trick or it was something else, but it damn well wasn't . . . Hell, I won't even say it! It's ridiculous.*

He violently pummeled his thoughts into a dark, forgotten cabinet in his mind, feeling stupid for giving any of this a second thought. He thought about what he'd say to Emily, the friend who'd set him up on this awkward date in the first place. Emily was never one to play many pranks, especially with a touchy dilemma like this. She knew that Brian was already skeptical when it came to relationships; so why would she go out of her way to ultimately hurt Brian this way? To shove it in his face that he was completely alone? It just wasn't like her at all.

Brian swung past his thoughts and past the door that led to the ramp, which led out to the real world. He sighed once more, dug his hands into his pockets, and got in his car. Then he drove home.

The next morning, at around noon, his friend Emily called. Brian was sprawled in bed, watching a program on his massive television set when he heard the phone ring. He answered it and felt a mix of emotions course through him.

"Hey!" she said cheerfully. "How was the date?"

Brian stiffened in bed. "It didn't work out," he said. He had planned to say something else—something more detailed, perhaps—but that was what came out first.

Emily was quiet on the other end. "Oh," she finally said. "That's too bad."

"Yeah," he said.

"Heather's a nice girl."

Brian felt his heart and stomach turn to a hollow pit at the mention of her name. He got a thought suddenly and it made him feel sick inside—*My soul mate might live in another dimension.*

That's ridiculous, another voice said. This voice filled with the simple wisdom of logical men, but sounding significantly weaker.

"Yeah," he said again. "She was nice. But do you think that . . . maybe . . ."

The receiver was silent.

"Maybe?" Emily echoed.

Brian sighed and felt the acrid thought float towards his mind again, but he forced it away.

"I don't know," he said. "Well . . . do you think she'd meet me again tonight?"

◖ All is Fair in Love

THE YEAR IS 1959. Hot weather. So hot that you can see the road glazed with bubbling heat at the end of the stretch. Driving with arched hands. Fingers jumping sporadically on the java-hot leather steering wheel. I swab the beads of sweat clutching at my face. Although I've tried it a hundred times before, I turn the air conditioner dial to its maximum setting with no result. Piece of junk car, I think. I drive a 1948 Studebaker that I purchased at an auction five years ago. It was a lovely heap of machinery when it was first made. Now it is a heap of junk on wheels.

On the passenger side of the car, a glass jar sits snug with the seat belt buckle clicked in around it. The jar has a sticker of tape with the words HANDLE WITH CARE scribbled in black ink. Occasionally, I will crane my neck to check on the jar.

"Almost there," I mutter to it. "First, I want to stop at the diner for a beer. Is that fine?"

The road curves and dips dramatically enough to see Hank's Diner just over a foothill. I park near the front entrance and the engine coughs before shutting off. I feel my chest expand as I step out of the car. A gust of cool air greets me.

Doorbell chimes.

"Morning, Hank," I say inside.

Hank regards me with a grimace. "Morning, Mr. Feltner."

I take a seat on a red vinyl stool and smile. "Fine day today."

"Is it?"

"Oh yes. Say, hand me a cold one, Hank."

Hank nods and slowly pours a glass of beer. The film of foam seems to float just above the glass, nearly spilling, until it gradually wanes.

As I drink it, I get the urge to smile again, but I'm too busy guzzling down the cold, bubbling beverage that I can't. After all that heat out there, though, the beer is just what I need. I let out a silent belch once I am satisfied.

"So like I was saying," —my near-empty glass thuds on the marble counter— "it's a damn fine day."

"A little too hot for my taste," Hank starts. "But humor me."

"The missus and I are going to West Palm Beach for the weekend."

"The missus." Hank stifles a laugh.

I grin in amusement. "Yes, Hank. The missus. Sandy. You've met, haven't you?"

Hank's smile fades. Now he is staring at me with what can only be pity.

He closes his eyes and shakes his head. "Jesus, Richard."

"It's going to be a memorable weekend indeed."

"Richard, maybe you should talk to someone. See someone about this," Hank says. "I know it's not my place and all, but . . . Jesus . . ."

My smile vanishes now. "Maybe you should show some Goddamn respect, Hank. I'm only asking for someone to be happy for me for a change."

I sip my last puddle of beer and slam the glass hard on the counter.

As I leave, I hear the doorbell chime before the morning sun drapes over me again.

◖

WHEN WE REACH the Olive Branch Resort, a valet attendant wearing a black hat nods and takes my keys. The lobby is a spectacle. A prideful chandelier hangs brightly over the scramble of men and women pacing the room. Their fancy dress shoes and high heels click and clap on the marble floor, making the room vibrant with bouncing echoes. A bellboy smiles at me and extends his arms out to take my precious jar. I shake my head.

"This is very fragile," I say to him. "Just take up my bags to room 811, please."

I hand him a crumpled dollar bill and he nods before taking it and leaving. The front desk is void of a line and I march up to it.

"Good morning, sir," a young woman with auburn hair says to me.

"Good morning," I say back. "I called earlier to reserve room 811."

"I remember," she smiles. She pinches up the rim of her glasses and writes something down. "Will you be alone?"

I straighten up. "No, ma'am. My wife Sandy will be staying with me, as well."

"Perfect," she grips the small hotel key and hands it over to me. "Have a swell stay, sir."

People begin to glance at my jar as I pass them by, and I can feel anger boil inside my cheeks and burn behind my eyes. Not today, I tell myself. This weekend is for Sandy.

Holding my jar, I open room 811 with the room key and my buttock, the door shutting alone as I place the jar on my bed. I twist and force the lid on the jar open. It makes a popping sound.

I smile. "There you are, sweetheart. I couldn't see you for a minute there. I was worried you had somehow escaped. But why would you, right? You're happy with me, aren't you? Why wouldn't you be?"

I lower my hand into the jar and stretch out a finger. The tiny ant moves chaotically around until it begins to climb my hand. I smile in adoration.

"Why wouldn't you be, Sandy?"

◖

SANDY AND I SPEND the remainder of the afternoon lounging in bed watching the ocean through the clear glass window. She's in a good mood today, I can tell. Something about the beach has always excited her.

After room service brings me my sandwich, I leave crumbs on the plate for Sandy. When I place her on the surface, she moves frantically in zigzags until settling on a morsel of bread for a few seconds. I have to be careful not to lose her. She is small but she is precious to me.

"Eat up," I say. "We have a big weekend ahead of us."

Down at the beach, the waves lap over the shore in ceaseless collisions. Beneath its roar lies the sound of children laughing while adults converse with restful ease. I skip over the sweltering sand in hurried hops, kicking up sand as I do so. Sandy is crawling on my hand. She's excited, I think. Oh yes, she is very excited.

I unravel a white towel with the words Olive Branch Resort sewn green in the fabric.

"Isn't this lovely?" I whisper to Sandy.

The black insect falters for a moment before continuing its blind race around my arm.

The sun's rays are just as piercing as they had been earlier in the Studebaker, but in the cool atmosphere and being shirtless, somehow it seems not only manageable, but therapeutic. I've been with Sandy long enough

—almost two months now—that I can sense her scuttling legs tickle the hairs on my skin even without looking.

I twist free a beer from a small cooler I brought with me and breathe deeply through my nose as the icy cold drink swims in its passage down to my stomach. After a few more beers, I plop onto the towel like a log. My eyelids begin to weigh down on me involuntarily. The bags under my eyes itch with fatigue. The sand beneath the towel makes a surprisingly pleasant pillow, and an unrelenting smile plays on my lips. I even manage to forget about Sandy for a moment.

Before I know it, I'm fast asleep.

◖

WHEN I AWAKE, the first emotion that succumbs my feeling of relaxation is panic. My arms dance and twist as I search for any indication of Sandy's whereabouts.

Nothing.

I stand gently and feel around the rough hairs on my neck, then the scruffy terrains of both my legs. My heart begins to throb heavily and my hands feel weightless. No, I think. Stupid! Stupid! How could you fall asleep? I stoop down to the towel as my eyes search warily in measured strokes. Just before I let out a loud cry (even in front of everyone at the beach), I finally see her. Sandy is crawling slowly on the towel. I let out an audible sigh.

"Thank heaven," I groan in relief. When I offer my hand, this time, Sandy doesn't hesitate to board it.

Some people nearby watch this whole scene unfold and raise their eyebrows in confusion. They don't understand, and I care not.

I walk us back to the hotel suite and, once inside, decide to sit on the bed.

"You gave me one hell of a scare," I say to Sandy. "You need to be more careful."

The ant is still.

"You're right," I say, depleted. "It was my fault. I shouldn't have dozed off like I did."

I grin widely as I observe her innocence. "I love you," I say.

The rest of the weekend plays out exactly as I had envisioned it. I'm much more careful now. Room service comes and goes, but other than that, we are pretty much left alone. I am happy. Sandy is happy. We find solace in each other's company and are finally rid of fools who look down on us. Sandy and I scarcely leave the room, and find our time dwindling away on board games and late-night talks. "Remember the time we went to Colorado?" I'd say. "Boy that was memorable, huh." Sandy would respond with a twitch of her antenna.

It is almost Sunday evening now, and I replay the events of the day in my mind. More memories made, I think in satisfaction. After I place Sandy in her jar again, I smile broadly at yet another successful vacation, even this time in Sandy's current state. My hands clench tightly in exhilaration, and joy swells up inside of me. It's just like it once was, the thought comes to me.

I release the grip on my hands leisurely, then my body stiffens. I look into the furrowed palm of my left hand and feel my throat catch. She never fell into the jar.

"Sandy?" I say barely audibly.

She isn't moving. And worse—her body seems disfigured and there is a clear liquid oozing from her remains.

"No," I whisper aloud. "No, no, no, no, no . . ."

Immediately, I'm seeing my hands shake through a dilated screen of tears, my mouth quivering in a broken frown. I spit out the ribbons of water flooding from my eyes and let out a hoarse cry. My love is gone.

Again.

◖

NOT LONG AFTER my check out, I drive back to my hometown. The drive is excruciatingly painful. The steering wheel remains fiery, but my numb hands don't feel a thing. My vision is blurred the whole way back. Before I know it, I reach my destination. I'm back in town, but I'm not home.

My car idles for a moment before I kill the engine. I pass the rusty gates and the flopping tin sign reading: Watermark Cemetery.

With each measured step, my legs wobble in rebellion. My tears are spent even when I reach the grave beside the great oak tree. I kneel down. The grass is sprinkled with dew and it is cold on my knees. I graze the bouquet of flowers I brought.

"For you," I say with a shaky voice.

With my free hand, I trace the crease of letters on the tombstone that reads the words :

SANDY FELTNER
1925-1959
LOVING WIFE, ETERNAL FRIEND
YOUR SPIRIT FINDS ITS WAY TO ME

I bow my head and find that I still have some tears left. I stroke the roses and then the grass of the earth. My shoulders give way as I slump down to my elbows.

"My sweet, my angel, my love," I say, weeping. "Where has your spirit gone now?"

A few seconds after I say this, a worm pushes itself out from the earth.

I smile and pick her up again.

◖ Next Flight Up

"WE GOT THE RICH SEATS," said Felicity, holding Grendel's hand.

Grendel smiled, knowing it was his daughter's way of suppressing her fear of flying. Everyone who was afraid had their own way. His, he decided, was drinking. But of course this time, with his family accompanying him, sleep would have to suffice.

"That's right, honey," he said.

Joan, his wife, gave him a dry look. She hated when their daughter made any public note of their wealth. *It's rude to those less fortunate,* she would have said, and was probably thinking.

Despite the lined-up crowd, they found their seats easily. Felicity sat in the middle.

"What type of plane is this, Daddy?" she asked as he buckled her in.

"A300."

"That's a good one?"

"The best, Honey."

Felicity nodded. Her legs kicked back and forth like offset pendulums.

"Let Daddy get by," Joan said.

Felicity held her scrawny legs back almost magnetically, and Grendel crossed to the window seat.

"Seat belts, please," said the stewardess. Almost simultaneously, a sign lit above the archway reading FASTEN SEAT BELT.

The stewardess approached their row and leaned over. "How's the little darling doing?" she asked. Grendel looked at Felicity, who wore a mask of apprehension on her face.

"Can you bring some water?" Joan said. "It's her first time."

The stewardess—her nametag read "Martha"—nodded.

She walked away and the engine started with a cough, and Grendel's head jerked left. He could see the fuselage rattling. Below, the propeller spun into a frenzied blur.

When the plane started moving, Felicity flexed her fist into a ball. Joan, his wife, reached for her hand. Grendel grabbed his daughter's hand as well, but more to snuff out his fears than for her sake. His fear of heights.

"We're all set, honey," Joan said, smiling.

"This is the fun part," Grendel added.

As the plane continued propelling itself forward, faster and faster, it slowly began angling itself toward the sun.

"Hawaii, here we come." Grendel could hardly hear himself.

The seats began to shake viciously as the plane leveled itself over the horizon. But something felt wrong. The plane wasn't high enough yet. Then it began to tilt downward.

The rest happened so quickly that Grendel couldn't register all of it. He didn't have time to even fully become afraid.

Felicity cried out in fear. Everyone in the plane was screaming, but for some reason he could only hear his daughter's pitchy squeal. Grendel could see thick, black smoke pumping from the engine. He was too stunned to move. The Pacific Ocean was a blue grim reaper below them, growing sharper and more vivid, as if its huge mouth was waiting like a shark to swallow the plane whole.

There was no time for an announcement—oxygen masks fell from above them. *Jesus,* Grendel thought. *This can't be happening.*

Felicity and Joan screamed, but nothing was heard anymore over the roar of the plane. As they came near the water, the plane skirted its surface and shifted upward, catching itself in a steadier drift. The plane wobbled shakily from left to right before beginning to ascend again.

We didn't crash, Grendel thought in a non-coherent trance. Turning, he noticed that the engine was fine; no more smoke was visible. How was it possible?

"Martha!" he yelled.

Felicity was crying; Joan paralyzed in fear.

The stewardess approached them holding a cup of water, but it wasn't Martha. "I believe this is for you," she said, handing the cup to Felicity.

"Where's Martha?" Grendel asked.

The stewardess, a young woman with pretty eyes, blinked those pretty eyes at him. "Martha survived," she said.

Grendel swallowed hard. "Sur—vived?"

"You've all been in an accident. Your plane crashed in the Pacific."

Felicity looked at her father, who was speechless.

"What are you talking about?" he asked. "What is this?"

The stewardess smiled. "You're going up. That's the good news."

"Up?" Grendel said.

The plane jolted, ascending in a powerful assault above the clouds, until they passed through the Mesosphere. As they reached outer space, their view darkened outside the windows and the Earth became a pale button behind them.

"Daddy, what type of plane is this?" Felicity asked.

Grendel gripped her hand. "I don't know, Honey," he said. "I don't know."

The Beat Matters

HIS HANDS WERE FLUTTERING up and down in panic. James could only hear the sound of his ragged huffs of breath. Panic attacks were normal for him, and as always, he was convinced that this time he would really die.

Breathe, breathe, he thought.

He was alone tonight. Part of him was glad for that—he couldn't bear (nor, he decided, could she) putting his wife through this again—while the terrified boy in him wanted nothing more than to have Justine by his side right now. Regardless, it was impossible. Her flight arrived tomorrow from New York; she was a world away.

He thought about calling her. Maybe she was still awake. The clock. No, you idiot! It's four-twelve! She needs her rest for tomorrow. By this point, James was already crossing his bedroom frenetically and nearly galloping towards the kitchen. He needed water. He needed to breathe slowly. This always passes. It will pass as always. He won't die. That's ridiculous.

Panic attacks can vary in intensity. Scarcely do they come in moderations. They are a tornado of fear that sweeps through a person with no warning or invitation. Blasts of unexpected adrenaline that came with, many times, the simplest negative thought. His palms would sweat, heart rate increase, body go numb, and it will almost always resemble a heart attack—James's greatest fear. Some days it would thrash his mood entirely, and often he would unjustly take his anger out on Justine. True, she couldn't possibly understand what he was going through, but she tried her best to support him. He knew that and it birthed guilt in him.

He ingested three bottles of water in less than two minutes, feeling cold strays dripping and flowing down his chin and neck. Water made him feel safer. Like he was giving his body what it ultimately needed. But that was the scare of it—he didn't know what it needed. He would just continue to breathe and drink, and wait it out.

Inhale. Exhale. Gulp. Inhale. Exhale. Gulp. Pace the room.

Slowly he could sense himself beginning to calm down. He sat down to cooperate with the shift in his body, letting relaxation move in. His heart wasn't racing anymore. Instinctively, he reached for his heart to check its velocity (it was a ritual he often did to further convince himself that everything was okay now). He pressed hard on his chest with his palm.

Harder.

No, he thought. *Impossible.*

Harder.

It's impossible. I'm not pressing it correctly. I'm dreaming. His panic returned in full force. Impossible. He choked his wrist and with trembling hands checked again and again for a pulse.

No. No, no, no, no, no.

He couldn't breathe. Every inhalation was like trying to lift a skyscraper bare-handed. *I'm imagining it. A heart only stops when you die*, he recited in his head. *Only when you die.* And yet . . . and yet . . .

James stood in the alien blackness of his kitchen, struck with fear and confusion. It was four-seventeen. He was sweating, breathing ragged huffs of breath. He was alive, but the heart inside of his chest had retired from beating.

THE FOLLOWING MORNING James refrained from phoning Justine; a temptation he almost couldn't snuff out. But it would only frustrate him more to have to explain this madness over the phone. And he would rather tell her in person anyway. He hadn't gotten much sleep; at some point he found himself dosing off, near sleep, but immediately the thought pounced back into his memory and he pressed his chest with a hard slap. Void.

You have no heaaaaart! A voice in his mind whispered. That's precisely how he'd heard it too. A demonic, heckling voice. Laughing at him in the darkness.

The sun was casting rays of light through his window now, and he could hear a bird whistling outside. Same damn bird as every morning. Typically it was a welcomed song, but today it sounded more like a cruel chuckle. The bird knew.

A concern swirled his mind—what would he tell Justine? How could she hope to understand? What doctor could remedy this absurdity?

James left his home and drove straight to the airport. The whole way there he felt like vomiting. The closer he got, it seemed, the more his nausea deepened. She was waiting for him just outside the terminal, and he helped her put the bags inside the back seat of the car.

"No hug first?" She outstretched her arms and gave a weak smile.

He hugged her, although he didn't want to.

"I'm sorry," he said. "I'm just tired."

"You slept bad? Another attack?"

"Yes." He didn't look at her as he stepped into the car. "And don't call it an attack. I'm fine. I wasn't attacked."

Justine lifted her arms in defense. "I'm sorry. You know what I meant."

"Let's just go. I'm tired."

They drove home and the car was silent all the way there. James noticed that the car needed gas, and a blinking light and ticking sound continued to remind him of this, but he couldn't imagine performing such a mundane task with this devil on his back. And so he drove on, even while Justine kept giving him petrified glances. He could see her in his peripheral, and his tongue clicked at his teeth in caged anger. *She won't understand you*, the mind-voice hissed. *She'll leave you in a heartbeat. Oh, wait, forget that last part, freak!*

"Shut up," he muttered lowly.

Justine craned her neck quickly. "Did you say something?"

"No," he grunted. "We're here."

James parked the car and began unloading her bags into the house. He hadn't even noticed that he'd left the door unlocked when he'd departed in the morning. Inside, the house was still.

"It's so good to be back," he heard Justine say from behind him. She moved into the kitchen and James heard cabinets shuffling open and closed. She returned into the living room and smiled weakly at him.

"What's wrong?" she asked.

"Nothing's wrong." Another lie.

She moved closer. "I missed you. So much. I don't want it to be like this."

Closer still. James dropped his head until his chin was almost touching his chest.

"Don't," he whispered.

"Don't what?" she pleaded, slowly inching towards him until her arms enveloped him.

James shook sporadically as she nuzzled her cheek against his chest. He didn't know whether to move or stay completely still. Would she notice that his heart wasn't beating? Could a person be so tuned to that? He decided that even if she did find out, it might be simpler than having to tell her himself. She would think he was joking if he tried that. Oh, as if he would joke about such a thing! He had to say it. He had to. He could be dying. James felt on the verge of another panic attack, and he suddenly pushed away from her. He briefly felt her hot breath through the thin fabric of his shirt as she gasped at the shove.

"James?" she spoke softly.

"Something is wrong with my heart," he said.

She met his eyes. Her eyes searched him until he felt weary and scared. "What do you mean?" she asked.

James only swallowed, his eyes unblinking.

She looked down at his socks, then looked up at him again. Then she stamped her hand against his chest. Again, James's tongue was immobile and incapable of words.

She waited a moment, her eyes unfocused on his chest, then said: "What is this?"

He wanted to shrug, but had no strength to do so.

"I . . . James, I can't feel your heart beating. What—what is this?"

"I don't know."

"What do you mean you don't know?" her voice rose. "What happened? What is this?"

She persisted to press his chest harder until he flinched back in pain.

James swallowed and began to pace the room. He always did that when he was nervous. Or when he felt another panic attack coming on.

"Is that *normal?* What the hell is this?" she cried.

"Last night," he recited in a clutter of words. "A panic attack came. My heart . . . my heart."

Another dry swallow. "I went into the kitchen. Water. Then I got water."

He could see that Justine was doing her best to listen without reacting in a way that might send both of them off the deep end.

She stopped him, waving her arms. "It doesn't matter, James. We need to see someone."

He stopped and sat down. "Sit with me." A frightened plea.

Justine sat beside him and began to caress his hair. She started to cry. "What do we do? What does this mean?"

He shook his head.

She looked ahead at the coffee table and sighed.

"I've never even heard of such a thing. But . . . you're alive," she said.

"I'm scared."

"Baby, let's take you to the hospital. Let's go right now."

"I'm scared," James repeated, and this time his face melted like a scared-stiff child with tears rushing down his face.

"Let's go now. Right now. They'll fix this." Justine got up from the couch and hurried into the kitchen to retrieve the car keys. James heard them jingle in her hand. He got up and wobbled to the door, feeling as though he were floating between rooms. The light outside was so bright that he had to walk with his hand against his face, only to see through the slits between his fingers. He thought he would collapse before he reached the car, but he didn't. The entire ride to the hospital—which was maybe fifteen minutes—was a blur. Only minutes in a person's life, but feeling more like a lifetime in itself. He heard Justine talking the whole way there, but she sounded muffled, like something he heard through a cement wall.

"Did you hear me?" she asked, penetrating his spell.

"What?" he blinked. "No, I'm sorry. Repeat it."

"I asked if you felt any different."

James thought about it. Aside from the shock of it and his usual sensation of panic, he didn't.

"I'm just nervous that the doctor might tell me something bad," he finally answered.

"Bad? Bad like what?"

He scoffed, playing the scenario in his head. The idea made him shiver. "Bad like bad," he finally said. "Bad like . . . 'James, you should be dead.' "

◖

JAMES WAS SITTING with Justine in a waiting room after the doctors had performed some tests on him. It wasn't the waiting room they were in at first. This one didn't have any magazines or a television set. Nor, as a matter of fact, did it have other patients. They were alone now. The room only had pamphlets. James didn't want to look at them. Pamphlets on heart disease, liver disease, brain disease, all kinds of diseases. Disease-disease-disease!

"Put that down," James ordered.

Justine lowered the pamphlet in her hands. "I'm just checking if any of your symptoms are—"

"I said put the damn thing down!"

She did as he demanded with stiff, even eyes. She crossed her arms and they sat in silence. The ticking of the clock sounded louder by the second, and the cold air smelled of medicine and rubber.

"This isn't easy for me either, you know," Justine said.

"I know," James replied.

"I'm trying my best to help and keep you calm."

"I know, Justine. I already said I know. I'm sorry. I'm just nervous about what they're going to tell me."

"Tell us."

"What?"

"Nervous about what they're going to tell *us*," she corrected him. "This is my dilemma too. I love you. And your problem will always be my problem, as well."

At that moment, a nurse walked into the room. She had green scrubs on, and her brown hair was tied in a bun. "James, Doctor Gale is ready to see you. Your wife can come too."

They followed the nurse out of the room. It felt as if his legs were marching on without his consent. His mind was still at home. Somewhere in the past, on a day when things were normal. How had this occurred?

They shifted through a maze of hallways before the nurse motioned for them to enter a double door. This door was different from the rest. It wasn't white with large gridded windows like the others; it was mahogany with no glass. It was an office.

Doctor Gale greeted them from behind his desk, also mahogany.

"Please, sit down," he gestured with his hand.

Justine immediately stopped. "Why? Will this take long?"

James looked at her oddly.

"Ma'am, please," Doctor Gale said. "Just have a seat."

They both did. James felt his eyes crossing, as if the vision of his independent eyes were merging into one distorted photo.

"Well?" Justine asked. Lucky for James, because he couldn't utter a single word.

Gale pursed his lips into a tight line. "I'm just going to be forthright." He lifted his hands in a gesture of surrender. "James's condition is rare, to say the least. No, more than rare—it's like nothing we've ever seen before. His heart isn't just at a fragile state, it's completely dead tissue. There's no blood pumping through it, and yet James is here with us, breathing and walking and talking. All his other organs are perfectly healthy too. But as you obviously know, a person can't live without their heart. I don't mean to alarm you, because as of now there's nothing to be worried about—nothing we've detected, at least—but son, you should be dead."

James tried to swallow but couldn't. He could see Justine's closed hand move over her mouth.

"But you're not," Gale added quickly. "And that's what's important. As of now, besides your heart, of course, we don't see any danger sneaking up on you. You're healthy as any normal person. It's a mystery, to say the least."

Before any of them could respond, Doctor Gale went on.

"Now, given these spectacular circumstances, we would like to keep you here for several days to run some more tests. Not only to be thorough, but for the advancement of the medical field in general. This could be a breakthrough in medicinal science. Of course, this would be completely free for you. It would be an honor for us."

"You want to experiment on my husband?" Justine said, appalled. "For science?"

"That's a minor detail, miss," he reassured her. "We would be helping him. It's important that we discover what exactly is keeping your husband alive. This is the best way to know for sure what's happening to him."

"I'll do it," James finally spoke out. "Just find out what the hell is going on."

◖

JAMES WAS TREMBLING CONVULSIVELY in his bed just before a nurse rushed in to his aid. She almost slid across the tile. Justine was waiting outside but ran in after her.

"What's wrong?" Justine cried out.

The nurse seemed preoccupied with machines. James appeared as though he were trying his best to hinder his shaking.

"It's nothing," she finally answered. "He was asleep and he woke up frightened."

Justine pulled up a chair beside his bed and grabbed hold of his arm.

James bit his lip. "I'm ff—fine," he said, quivering.

It was turning on the third day since James had been detained in the hospital. Each day a new test was conducted, and each day a new doctor arrived to examine this wonder of a man. The living man with no heartbeat. *Three days*, James wondered, *and no hint of an answer.*

Justine was advised to leave the room as soon as the doctor entered.

"Gale," James murmured.

Doctor Gale walked in with a syringe in hand. "Here you go. Now, this is some stronger stuff for you. Lorazepam. Big word, I know. It's just Ativan; that's an easier name. Might put you out for a bit. Do you have any medical conditions I should know about?"

James almost said that he was prone to serious panic attacks, but then decided against it. *He wouldn't take me seriously if I told him that*, he thought. He needed the shot to relieve his anxiety.

James shook his head. Before he could rethink the thought, the needle cut into his skin and fluid swam deep into his arm, pricking his vein.

"Good," Gale said. "Then you're going to love this stuff. You'll be in heaven."

James tried to speak. He only mumbled something indistinct as his eyes flickered around the room.

◖

AS THE NEXT FEW DAYS came and went, so did with them a crowd of students from different universities, hovering over James, inscribing notes. They scribbled above him and squinted their eyes to get a more focused look at the readings of the cardiac monitor as if he were a lab rat. The leads were stuck to his chest like soul-sucking worms, delivering the dreadful message to the machine. The message that whoever is being checked right has no pulse. Is dead. There was no heart rate. There was no rhythm. Just the constant beep one hears when their loved one has passed. Yet James was still breathing, eyes open, watching the faces of these young students. They looked amazed. *Look how amazing I am!* thought James comically. Anger and annoyance seized him. Where was the progress? Where was the promise?

The sedative kicked in instantaneously and James began to chuckle as Justine came in.

He laughed and slapped his thigh.

Justine didn't look the least bit amused. "What's so funny?"

He continued laughing hysterically. Louder and louder.

"I cheated death!" he bellowed. "Doesn't that deserve a good laugh? I cheated death and I cheated these stupid doctors! They don't know what they're doing!"

"James, *enough.*" Her eyes were rigid.

"Why? What can they do to me? What can anyone do?"

The students continued their writing. They scribbled faster now, as if his maniacal reaction gave some sort of clue to the mystery of his case.

"That's enough, James. Get some rest. You're drugged up."

He was way ahead of her. He remembered these thoughts before falling asleep: *Funny. Scribble on, fools. May not wake up again. No heart for it.*

◀

WHEN HE AWOKE, Justine was outside of the room doing more paperwork. She did it almost every day. James was watching television when he suddenly felt his mouth go dry as wood. He felt his hands shaking again.

"Nurse," he called, pressing a button beside his bed. It didn't seem to be working. Light wasn't on as usual.

"Great," he murmured. He tried and failed to sit upright on the bed. In an instant, his arms buckled beneath his weight and he collapsed on the mattress. All he could see through his vision was the television set playing some sitcom. An uncontrollable fear devoured his entire body and he felt a cold chill sweep through him. It was as if his limbs weren't connected to his body. Another panic attack blasted in him like a sudden earthquake. He slapped his heart, craving a pulse, craving any sign that he was really alive. Oh the dead nothingness! Oh the void! Give me something! he wanted to scream. But he couldn't. He didn't dare utter a word. James reached out to grab the same syringe the doctor had used earlier. He had forgotten the name of it, but he didn't care. When did he take his last shot? he wondered. How long was he asleep?

Didn't matter. The fear was overwhelming.

On instinct, James found a dark pink vein on his arm and pushed in the needle. In less than a minute, he felt his body relax. He lay on the bed trying to regain his breath when he heard a crackling sound near the wall. He looked and saw the lamp plug fly out of the wall socket with electrical sparks shooting forth from it. Then the room got consumed by shadows and the volume on the television increased until it was shouting at him, making his ear drums tremble. James covered his ears and squeezed his eyes shut.

"I'm imagining it," he shouted over the noise. Why did I take that shot? What the hell was I thinking?

His legs were asleep as he stood up, and a thousand fiery needles danced through the fibers of his muscles. He had to sit back down. Then he rose again. He wobbled over to the door and could overhear people talking in the other room.

"—tough love," he heard a voice cry out in laughter. "Poor bastard."

Other voices laughing. They sounded like chipmunks. "Must've been one hell of a heartbreak, for his heart not to work! Talk about depressing."

More chipmunk laughter. "I wonder what else doesn't work."

More laughing. He stumbled back. He couldn't believe it—they were joking about him. He didn't want to listen anymore. But he could still hear the laughing. It sounded like the sitcom laugh-track behind him. Was this how they were spending their—his—time? Making jokes about his condition!

James grew furious and returned to his bed. Those fools! Taking his anguish lightly. His frustration. He was sick of being a lab rat, sick of being the occasion for mockery. He walked up to the door again and planned on complaining when he heard a familiar voice from within the group.

"Well, Gale, in answer to your last question," Justine said, "his performance in the sack is pretty dead too."

Hysterical laughter.

James drove a closed fist into the wall and grabbed a large scalpel from the table. He rushed out of the room and met the crowd.

"You bastards!" he shrieked.

Justine ran to him. "Baby, you shouldn't be out of bed!"

"Don't you dare!" he yelped. "I hate you!"

Doctor Gale extended his arms. "James, get back to bed."

"So you can mock me again? I don't think I will."

"Who's mocking you?" Justine cried out.

"Ah, who? I heard you! Laughing about my dead heart like I'm some poor bastard. Talking about my—my—"

"You're not lucid," Gale said. "Your eyes. Jesus, did you inject yourself?"

"You're the poor bastards! All you heart-dependant idiots!" James raised his arm high to the ceiling, blade in hand. "I'll outlive you all with my 'disease'! Put that in your medical books!"

"He's foaming," Justine cried to Gale. "His mouth!"

James ripped off his hospital gown and was completely naked in front of the small group of nurses and the doctor, and his wife.

"See?" he screeched. "I don't need this."

He lowered the blade and dug it into his chest until blood began spewing out.

"Oh my God!" they all screamed.

James was laughing uncontrollably as flesh toppled over his stomach, mixed with blood and guts. The gaping hole in his chest was growing larger with each scrape and scoop, until he snapped two of his ribs bare-handed and literally stabbed his heart right out of his chest. It was a wet, red blob of a ball, dripping fresh blood on the tile.

Two of the nurses fainted. Justine hadn't stopped screaming.

"James, no!" Gale pleaded.

"Ha! I'll outlive you all! This heart is a calloused dead lump to me!"

James pushed through the crowd and ran out of the hospital. Justine almost fainted while begging the hospital security to catch him.

"We're contacting the police," one of the uniformed men said. "They'll find him."

"Alive," she added.

"Yes, of course," he turned. "Alive."

PANIC ATTACKS CAN VARY in intensity. Scarcely do they come in moderations. They are a tornado of fear that sweeps through a person with no warning or invitation. Your palms sweat, heart rate increases, body goes numb, and it will almost always resemble a heart attack—James greatest fear.

James would never have to worry about such things anymore. It had been a strange week for him. As he sprinted down the dark sidewalk, he thought about Justine. God, he loved her. He needed her.

But he was alone tonight. Part of him was glad for that, while the terrified boy in him wanted nothing more than to have her by his side right now. Regardless, it was impossible.

Damn it. Stupid drug, he thought. He knew it was the shot that caused this. Why did this have to happen to him? He didn't want to be a part of this phenomenon any longer. Still, he continued running. He ran in fear. Ran in blind fury. Ran because his legs were already in the process.

The police search for him continued for nearly an hour, until James was found dead on his kitchen floor, a pool of blood around him, naked with an empty bottle of water in his hand.

◖ Wake Up!

"MR. HARKINS."

There's a steady pounding somewhere nearby.

"Mr. Harkins!"

And then I wake up. I'm in my office in New York.

"Coming," I say. I swipe at the drool on my chin and rub it off on my black pants. In a matter of seconds, I manage to compose myself, tucking in my shirt. I open the door.

My subordinate, the finance director, Darryl, hands me a thick green folder. "Damn it, Franky. It's twelve twenty. The meeting started at twelve, remember? How long do you think they'll be willing to wait for you?"

I wiggle my tie into place. "All day. All day, if they have to." I'm half-kidding, but it's true. I'm the CFO and it's a finance meeting.

"You're wrong, Frank. Let's get going, please."

We exit the room and turn into the conference room down the hall. A small crowd of faces stares me down. Among them is the company's owner, Kenny Dodge.

We shake hands. "Frank," he says in greeting. His painful grip makes me wince.

"Kenny," I say, smiling forcibly. "Sorry for the wait."

"Nonsense." We all sit and a few of us shuffle through our files.

Kenny Dodge speaks first. We discuss our dwindling stock value and the decline of our profits over the last six months. Our sub-Saharan African laborers, Mr. Dodge explains, are the main cause of this. The medical attention they require far outweighs their productivity. In short, Dodge suggests we stop supporting them like mother geese and—he sugar-coats this, of course—suck them dry.

I cringe in discomfort. Nobody seems to notice.

Darryl looks at me for permission to speak.

I shake my head, no. "Is this the only solution?" I ask.

Kenny chuckles, drumming on the table lightly with his finger. "You remind me of my boy, Charlie. Always going against the grain."

He avoids my question and, before long, everyone has left.

I go home late into the evening and kiss my wife, walk up the stairs of my luxurious home, and seclude myself in the master bedroom of my mansion. The canopy bed calls me, as always, to silent reclusion. It seems to be smiling a grin of purpose and death. It shows its teeth in the contours of the bronze railing. I sigh and sag into the bed sheets, my soul slinking away. My being drifting away.

◖ TWO: MWAMUILA

I AWAKEN IN AFRICA. My dark skin is hardly visible in the windowless room. The only light I see is coming from some hole in the roof. My name is Mwamuila now. The next time I wake up, it will be Frank Harkins again. My life has been this way ever since I can remember.

Frank's father was a CFO in New York, and when he died from cancer four years ago, Frank was promoted to take his place. His father had been grooming him for the position for years.

I wasn't so lucky. The only thing my Baba owned was the skin glued to his bones, and with that he did more good in a day than Frank's father ever did in his lifetime. My Baba died of a disease I've never heard of. Maybe it was cancer as well. Who knows? And aside from Mama and my sister and me, who cares? People die here every day.

I walk out into the searing sunlight, shielding my eyes with rigid, crusty fingers. Looking over, I see what I expect: my neighbors' feet shuffling across the poorly-paved ground, sandals making the sound of sandpaper on a chalkboard.

I walk across to where Mama is with my younger sister at the school. I find them both on the porch. I wave and smile in the sun.

"Did you just wake up?" Mama says to me in Swahili.

"Yes, can you believe it?" I respond.

She purses her lips to indicate that she can.

My sister, Adilah, hides behind Mama's leg. She is already eight, but still a shy little girl in almost every way. Mama sees that Adilah is sucking her thumb again and slaps her shoulder like a paddle slaps water. Adilah doesn't cry. She rarely does. Her thumb only slips like a wet cork from her mouth.

Mama knows about my Frank Harkins dreams. She's known since I was a small boy. I would often—practically daily—crawl into her cot and tell her about the boy who took over my life every night. "He possesses me," I would say, weeping. I would tell her about his white skin and the large home he lives in.

In the beginning, she dismissed my stories as nightmares or cries of neglect. But as I got older, I was able to describe to her things that she had never known as a poor African—descriptions of a home that I couldn't have invented in my mind, toys that I couldn't have ever owned or even heard of—and when one morning I recited to her a speech in English that Frank had memorized earlier that week, I could see Mama's jaw drop and her eyes sink back in horror.

For months, she invited spiritual leaders from our village to puzzle out what demon was holding my mind captive. They chanted prayers over my head and made vain attempts to cast out evil spirits. But I knew that this was my life from the beginning. I knew it wouldn't work.

◖ THREE: FRANK

THE NEXT MORNING at the office, I call Darryl into the room. He comes through the door and shuts it. I look up at him. "We can't let them abuse those people anymore," I say.

Darryl coughs a laugh. "What can we do?"

"I'm still working on that. I just need you to back me up."

I can already tell he isn't pleased with my request.

"Frank," he starts, "Frank, this is a business. A failing one at that. You gotta let them do their job. You can dish out that it's immoral—evil, even—but nobody's blaming you. No one is pointing fingers and saying it's your fault."

I'd known he wouldn't understand; I was prepared for his response. Not prepared with a comeback, but enough so that I don't lash out in anger.

"Just say you'll support me." My hands shake as I light a cigarette.

He sighs and shrugs just enough to let me know that he'll try. I nod and he leaves the room.

◖ FOUR: MWAMUILA

WHEN BABA DIED a few years ago, I was forced to take up a job that could support Mama and Adilah. Frank saw this and researched the nearest location where his company had low-paid laborers, and I began my work there. It hasn't solved all of our problems, but like a

Band-Aid on a bleeding war wound, it suffices for the time being.

One of the bigger problems is the distance. I have to walk six miles every day. The heat is oppressive; it took its toll on me long ago, but though my mind rebels, my feet keep me going.

Now, unsure whether Frank can change his boss' mind, I begin to worry. I don't tell Mama, because she is too old to spend her last years in constant anxiety for our future. If it gets bad, I will simply tell her that relocating is a good option.

Of course, finding another job will be close to impossible in this season of the year, when our people are all in great need of help.

This season? Who am I kidding?

The sun is going down. In our small, dirty room, Mama serves us oatmeal in small bowls. We've split a single apple three ways. Mama smiles at me and, after we pray, she begins to eat the oatmeal feverishly. All the while, Adilah is looking at me with sad eyes. I smile at her and she turns away. A chill crawls up my shoulders, and I take a bite from my apple slice.

◖ FIVE: FRANK

I CATCH KENNY DODGE just as he's packing up to leave. He smiles and tosses his leather messenger bag over his shoulder. "What can I do you for?" he says.

"I wanted to speak with you about what you said earlier. About our African laborers."

He frowns, because this isn't the first time I've brought it up.

"It's important."

He raises an eyebrow. "Is it now?"

"Yes. Very."

"That doesn't strike me as surprising. What I do fail to understand, however, is why the hell you care about our laborers in Africa so much. We give them work—isn't that enough?"

Why do I care about them? His question resounds in my mind, even as he continues to speak. I don't have a reasonable answer except, of course, that I've spent half of my life in Africa. What other choice do I have than to care? It's the dread of tomorrow that fills me with sorrow today. Inescapable, looming dread that threatens a chronic existence if I don't act soon.

When Mr. Dodge chuckles, it calls back my attention. "Anyway," he says, "it damn well better be. It *has* to be. We're not responsible for their health."

"They work overtime, Kenny. If they lived in America, their health would be our responsibility. Why should it make a difference?"

"Dammit, Frank! I'm sick of this. It's a no, you got it? A *no*. Please just drop it before this gets out of hand."

I feel my heart pump faster and my cheeks get red hot. "I have family there," I blurt out. It's a mistake, but I am angry and I run with it.

"Excuse me?"

"That's right," I say, hoping to God he doesn't catch me in my lie.

His face pales behind growing eyes. "What the hell are you talking about?" he says. "Your parents were both from Jersey. And both were white."

I blink. "It's hard to explain," I mutter.

He looks disappointed in me. I can feel it like a boy about to be sent to his room without supper, only the consequences for my actions will be more severe.

"There's nothing I can do, Harkins," he says finally. "Listen, I have a family to worry about, too. My wife. My son, Charlie." He pulls out his wallet to show me a picture. A young, freckle-faced blond boy smiles through the plastic insert. "This is *my* family, Frank. This is *my* boy, *my son.* I have to think about him first, don't I?"

When I see that he expects an answer, I nod.

"Damn right," he says, then he lowers his head. "Look, buddy. Between you and me, my family is going through some financial problems, too. Don't let the fancy suit fool you. This is work attire, and I have to dress the part, you know? Charlie, though . . . he isn't doing so great right now. I just have a lot on my mind, so I'm sorry if I'm being blunt with you. I just hope there's a mutual respect in the end. Our business needs this, though." Kenny pats my shoulder. "I just can't change my decision for your distant relatives." He gives me a look of pity before walking away.

Distant relatives, I think distastefully, bitterly. *Distant. Oh,* that's *rich.* That's *a laugh.*

That's real rich.

◖ SIX: MWAMUILA

MAMA IS DYING. For months, her heart has been getting weaker at a noticeable rate. And now, I don't need doctors to tell me she doesn't have long.

I kneel beside her bed, refilling her cup of water and humming the melody of a song I learned when I was a boy. A song Frank taught me.

Mama can't hear me. Her eyes are fixed to a point on the ceiling as her stomach swells with every inhale and exhale.

"Drink," I whisper.

She does so after a few seconds; her shaky hands rising up to grab the cup like a fragile stem growing from the dirt.

I love Mama. I don't want her to die.

Adilah peeks into the room, and I tell her to go back outside. When she goes, I follow her, slowly closing the door behind me.

"Is she going to die?" Adilah asks.

"No," I say.

Adilah nods and looks at her fingers. "I had a new vision."

For years, Adilah has been getting visions. In just about all of them, an evil person was holding a rope and tugging it with dark power while Baba and Mama tried to hold on. The evil man wore shadows for a face and his body was eating away all the light around him.

Baba was always holding the other end of the rope, his bare feet sinking deeper into the dirt with each forceful pull. Behind him was Mama, chucking up sand with her feet as she tried to find stability. They didn't have the power to pull back, only to hold on for their lives.

The evil man would laugh, Adilah said, and he would laugh even harder when Mama would trip and stumble to the ground, until Baba screamed for his life and was absorbed into the darkness of the evil man's body.

Baba died shortly after this was recounted to me. I never mentioned it to anyone. If the visions were more than mere coincidences, it meant that Mama was only a few feet behind, still clutching the rope.

"What was the vision this time?" I ask Adilah, fearing the answer I somehow know.

She begins to cry in dreadful sobs, shielding her face with her hands. Her fingers slip over her wet face.

"You were behind Mama," she says between sobs. "And I was behind you."

When I go back to the room to check on Mama that evening, she is dead.

◖ SEVEN: FRANK

I WAKE UP SICK AT HEART. I am sick of this. May God forgive me, but I am sick of it. What's the use of being successful when, half your life, you suffer the same fate as a poor man? My whole life has been this paradox: that no matter how rich or successful I become, my fortune is like jewelry adorning a dead man. I am plagued by this curse, and it's making it impossible to enjoy the fruits of my real life.

For the next couple of weeks, I try to set up a plan where I can send money to Mwamuila and Adilah. The plan fails sooner than I expect. The border issues, the customs, the currency changes, the remoteness of Mwamuila's village, the lack of financial infrastructure —it seems impossible.

In any case, I realize that supplying money to his family was never a solution, even if it were possible. The current grief of Mwamuila's life is only the symptom of a disease. There is no point in treating the symptoms when the disease lives on.

I tell myself that I've tried. I've really tried.

But now my dwindling options leave me with no other choice.

I have asked for a week of vacation. I pack my things, among them my .50 caliber Desert Eagle, and purchase my ticket to Africa. I don't expect to be gone long, but I pack some extra clothes just in case.

The airport is crowded when I arrive. Airport security looks over my gun closely, but I have packed it properly. On the other side, I am sure I will have to pay a bribe to leave the airport with it. Not an issue.

I board the plane. Breathing is an effort.

God forgive me, but I am sick of it.

◖ EIGHT: MWAMUILA

I WAKE WITH A VIOLENT GASP and find Adilah watching me. Frank must have fallen asleep on the plane. He will come for me soon.

Last night Adilah and I buried Mama at the cemetery. It was nice to see some of her old friends show up. I know she was smiling down from heaven. Felt it in the way the stars shone.

That peace is gone now. I must stay awake long enough to hide myself and Adilah. But even if I do, won't Frank just know where we are and come looking for me? Of course he will. Anyway, I must try. At least for Adilah's sake. She can't survive on her own. I know it.

I come up with a plan as I am putting Adilah's things in a bag to leave. Frank won't know where we're hiding because I myself won't know. If I blindfold myself and let Adilah guide me, he won't know which way she's leading me. It will work!

I tell Adilah and she nods bravely.

"I'll do as you say, Mwamuila," she says.

I smile at her and take her tiny hand after I tie a shirt over my face. I feel Adilah's hand jerk mine slightly and I follow. Soon, the only giveaway that I'm outside is the sun heating my shoulders. I smile again in satisfaction. My plan is a good one.

"Spin me," I tell Adilah. "I know you're going east. Remember to make sure you take me somewhere we've never been."

I begin to spin and she flaps her hands rapidly against my waist to help turn me. I laugh out loud for the first time in weeks, and I hear her high-pitched giggle move around me. Even under the shade of the wrapped shirt, I notice the light change from absolute black to bright black as I spin. When she stops me, I stumble before regaining my balance.

"Okay," I say, exhausted. "Continue."

She leads me in a blind, winding path for about an hour. When I am too tired to go on, we stop.

"Ready," she says.

"You sure?"

She hesitates. Then, "Yes!"

I undo the knot of my shirt and slip it over my thick hair. The light is blinding, and at first I can't even make out Adilah's sun-lit face. Her sweaty black skin looks golden in the sunlight.

She did a good job of hiding us; I have no idea where we are. I spin again and see only scrub trees, sparse grass, and sand. Good.

Scary, but good.

Adilah and I set up camp as the sun hides under the earth's shell. Frank must be on our trail by now. Once I'm asleep, I'll know for sure.

We cook and eat a dead bird we find; it was dead when we found it, but it looks fresh. As I'm finishing, I can feel my eyelids begin to sag.

Once the fire is safely out, I collapse heavily to the ground.

◖ NINE: FRANK

THE PLANE HAS LANDED. It's about damn time, too. I slept most of the way and it was still unbearable.

I move to luggage claim and find my things. In order to keep my gun, I pay the expected bribe to a large African guard.

From years of living in Mwamuila's reality, I already know exactly where to find his home. It is in a small village near Merca in Somalia. I need only find my company's facility where he works, then take the same six-mile walk he makes every day. Except I arrange for a taxi to get me to the place.

When a white, weathered coupe rolls into the airport, I climb in. The seats feel like burnt slabs of meat, and the man behind the wheel knows little English. But he knows enough. At least enough to understand what left and right mean—or maybe he is only following my pointing finger.

The muggy ride to Mwamuila's town is bumpy and awkward. As we ride, I reach into my suitcase and finger the trigger of my gun. I've never shot a man before—but I won't be shooting someone else, will I? No, I'll be shooting myself. The "self" of me that is a cancer to my success and my happiness.

Under the primitive circumstances, I survive the ride. I pay the man his fare and tip him fifty dollars. Till now, he hadn't cracked a smile. Now he's beaming hotter than the sun on my back. Money can't buy happiness, my ass.

When I reach the village—I know I've arrived because tin shack houses litter the sandy field and the air smells of festering skin—I try to remember what I can from my dreams. I find Adilah's school soon enough, the poorly constructed house peeking over a brown hill. The sight brings an unexpected sense of nostalgia. I'm finally in that dream place. It feels like worlds colliding.

I ignore my sentiments and focus on my mission. I can't let emotions get in the way. This other life has plagued me for too long.

There it is. Mwamuila's hut.

Of course it's there. I shouldn't be surprised, but I can't stifle the smile on my face. Is it any wonder? I both love and hate this place. I love it for the dream-like sentiment it gives me now, and I hate it for other, obvious reasons.

For a moment, I worry, as I have for days now, that if I kill Mwamuila, maybe I'll die as well. That somehow our life lines are linked. It wouldn't be too outrageous a notion, considering the circumstances. But I remember that when Mwamuila almost died of an immensely high fever—we were seven at the time—my own health wasn't affected at all. Does that mean something? I'm not sure, but I won't let that stop me.

I can't go on living with him.

The hut is empty, as I expected, but I look at the dirt and find what I hoped to find.

Footprints.

Those fools didn't think to hide them. Two sets of footprints mark a trail that leads into the scrub. I follow it. Even with the scrubby trees, the ground is mostly sand, and the trail remains clear. I follow it for nearly an hour until I see something interesting.

Yes.

I find their old fire.

They're here somewhere. They're—

❰ TEN: MWAMUILA

I AWAKE TO SEE Adilah crying, slouched by a tree. My heart quakes in fear when I see, like a doll lost in the dirt, Frank Harkins. Adilah is holding a large log and it drops to the ground. She cries harder.

"What happened?" I say.

"He was going to get you."

I look at the log. "And you . . ."

Adilah nods.

"You did the right thing," I say.

The sight of Frank on the ground makes me feel disoriented, like an out-of-body experience. There on the ground is half of my life. The half I wish I could experience all the time, with Adilah by my side.

And then it hits me.

I suddenly have it. The solution, the compromise. The way I can give Frank what he wants, and give Adilah what she needs. Of course! Now that I know it . . . Now that I know, it makes perfect sense. How to save Adilah. To save her from the shadow man in her visions.

I approach Frank's curled body slowly, knowing what must be done. Adilah hides behind me, digging her wormy nails into my leg. I lean over and reach for Frank's gun. It is black and heavy in my hand.

I raise the gun to my temple. Adilah screams.

I know that when I awake as Frank Harkins again, I'll be in paradise. This time, even in my sleep.

This time with Adilah.

I can finally rest.

◖ELEVEN: FRANK

I HEAR THE EXPLOSION of the gunshot as my eyes snap open. And Adilah's shriek makes my heart scream almost as loud. I scamper to cover her mouth with my hand, her voice becoming a muted alarm beneath my cupped palm.

"Quiet!" I whisper to her.

Of course, she doesn't understand me. I don't speak Swahili, but apparently *quiet* means *bite*, because that's what Adilah does. I pull my hand back with a yelp, perplexed to see a large portion of my palm flesh bitten off. Blood floods over my entire hand and, through woozy eyes, I see Adilah spitting bloody skin to the dirt.

"Wewe aliuawa ndugu yangu!" she cries.

"I don't understand!"

"Wewe aliuawa ndugu yangu!"

I raise my hands and attempt to calm her down. "Please, Adilah. I'm here to take you home. It's what Mwamuila wanted."

Her crying stops. It's enough for me to relax, but I stiffen again when she lowers herself to Mwamuila's body and picks up the Desert Eagle.

Jesus, I think. "No, Adilah. Put that down. That's not a toy."

"Toy," she repeats. Then she smiles and points the gun at me. "Toy?"

"No!" I say. "Not toy. Give it to me."

Her little wild grin sends chills crawling on my back. She's going to kill me.

"You kill my brother," Adilah says.

"How?" I shrill. I'm confused. How can she speak English? Mwamuila never taught her. Not that I can remember, at least.

I must use this to my advantage if I want to live. I must reason with her. *Christ, that smile.* It's wretched enough to drive a man insane. Her eyes, fixed on me like the barrel of that gun. What can I say to end this?

"Please . . ." It's a weak start, but it's all my throat can utter. "I'm taking you back to New York with me. It's what Mwamuila wanted."

"No," Adilah says. "What you wanted."

She cocks the gun.

"No," I cry. "Jesus, no."

She smiles wider and takes a step back. Then farther back.

I wait for the gunshot, but it doesn't come. She walks into the trees until she disappears completely. I don't know why, but for some reason she has shown me mercy. I accept it, and I run.

Boy, do I run.

◗ TWELVE: FRANK

I'VE BEEN SLEEPING well for almost a week now. Really sleeping. The act will take some time getting used to, but right now I'm content just to know that there is rest available.

Do I miss Africa? I've been asking myself that question daily, and my answer is yes. Though I feel relieved overall, nostalgia creeps its way in still. I suppose that's to be expected.

It's bedtime. I brush my teeth and shower, looking forward to another full night of normal sleep. Black, unregistered bliss. I change into my pajamas and crawl into bed. I turn out the light. The room is a dark purple haven, the window showcasing the moon's ambient glow. My wife is at a dinner with her company and will be coming home late tonight. I usually wait up for her on these nights, but right now, I still have the excitement of a child given a new toy. A new toy that—

"Toy," a voice says in the darkness on the far side of the room. It is a child's voice.

"Hello?" My heart begins to rampage inside my chest. "Who's there?" *Jesus*, I think. Is it Adilah?

Impossible.

"Hello?" I say again.

As my eyes adjust to the darkness, I see a small figure pressed against the wall of my room. I can't make out the face, but it looks about Adilah's height.

She's come for me. But how? How could she leave Africa? It's impossible.

"Are you going to kill me?" I say.

The figure's head nods. I hear a gun click.

It isn't Adilah; I can see the hair end below the figure's ears, while Adilah had long, kinky hair. This child isn't black, either. The child is white. And I can see now that he's a boy.

The boy begins to emerge from the shadowy wall, and I can see the gun.

"Why are you here?" I say.

"To kill you."

I can't breathe. "Why? Please, God, why?"

"You killed Adilah's brother."

Christ Almighty. "Who are you?" I say.

The boy steps closer into the moonlight. I can see the boy's hair is blond now. And freckles layer his pallid face. And that smile.

I know that smile. I know this boy.

The boy is Kenny Dodge's son.

"Charlie," I whisper.

"Yes."

Everything makes sense now. No wonder Adilah knew how to speak English.

"But why?" I begin to cry.

"You killed Adilah's brother. She was too kind to do anything about it. I'm not so kind."

"I don't understand!" I am choking on my tears, almost amused at how broken and despicable my voice sounds. *This boy means to kill you*, my mind assures me. *There's nothing you can do.* "For God's sake, I don't understand!" I shout again.

"I think you do," little Charlie says, pointing the gun at me. "I really think you do."

I tremble against the headboard. Yes, maybe I do understand.

I hear the gunshot. Then fade into blackness, this time having nowhere else to wake up.

Late-Night Snack

MY DAD IS A GOOD DAD. He's always been good to me and my mom. Most of the times I mean. He plays baseball with me most of the time when I ask him, or sometimes even when I don't. I don't have to beg my dad to please play with me, like some of the kids in my class. They sometimes tell me that they have to beg and beg their daddies to play sports with them, like baseball or football. I beg my daddy sometimes, beg him till I'm crying with boogers or sometimes bleeding in my mouth.

But not for stuff like baseball. Not for stuff like that.

MY DAD IS A WORKING MAN. That's what my mom says I mean. I don't know what a working man does, but in the morning he's not there so my mom makes me breakfast and takes me to school. I go to the third grade. She doesn't like me riding on the bus because the kids talk bad about me there, and the bus driver doesn't do anything to stop it like my teachers at school. My teachers at least will tell the kids to leave me alone and mind their own beez wax. That always helps me a little.

Anyways, my mom is a housewife (that's what she tells me, but I don't know if that's a real job or not). She cleans and cooks and stuff like that, so I guess it's just like work. She just doesn't get paid like my dad does. Whatever my daddy does as a working man, he must do it real good cause we live in a pretty big house. I've been to my friend Lucas's house and it's a lot smaller. He has a tree house though, so I guess that makes up for the small house. I would trade the whole big house of mine for that tree house. I know it's a bad trade, but I feel safe when me and Lucas go there. We play board games or look at magazines that Lucas's dad keeps under his bed. His wife doesn't even know (if you read this and you know them, please don't tell. Lucas made me swear and I'm serious about that stuff). The magazines show girls —and I promise you that they're completely naked. Sometimes it's a little bit gross but still kinda cool.

I just wanted to tell you about my life so that I can tell you this next thing. It's something about my dad. I don't want you to think he's bad, because most of the time he's the best dad in the world.

But sometimes he's bad.

◖

MY NAME IS DENNIS. No, not Dennis the Menace, I never even saw that show. And don't even try to think of what rhymes with Dennis because I think it's only 'menace' (which is taken) and 'tennis,' and there's nothing funny about that. Dennis Donaldson, that's my name. My dad is Patrick Donaldson and my mom is Gloria Donaldson.

But this story is mostly about my dad, Patrick Donaldson. My dad always comes into my room in the night. At 2:15 in the night. Always that time. I don't know why. He's not awake when he does it though. His eyes are closed, so I don't think it's really him doing it. I'm recording the whole thing tonight on my voice recorder so that you can know what happens. It's scary to me, and I'm really scared that my dad means what he says when he comes at night and tells me he's going to kill me and eat me.

◖

IT'S 2:10 A.M. RIGHT NOW. My mom and dad put me to bed a bunch of hours ago, at 8 p.m. At that time it was just beginning to get dark outside, and starting to get a cold purple in my room. The small shadows were just being eaten up by bigger shadows, and then even bigger shadows ate up those until the whole room was just one fat sticky shadow coming off the walls.

My Spiderman poster was always the first to get swallowed up by the dark, and sometimes from my bed I waved the poster goodbye. Tonight I did earlier too, but that was earlier. I slept a little, but my body is so used to waking up at this time that it wakes up by itself now—like if my brain is giving me a warning that my dad is gonna come soon.

It's 2:14, he's almost coming. Oh I'm really scared, shaking and colder than I'm supposed to be. My blankets must be invisible, like I'm grabbing nothing but air. I have to whisper lower now so I can hear better.

I can hear the floor squeaking, like a grandma crying in the other room. It sounds far down the hall, but it's coming closer. The wood floor sounds like it's connected to each other with fat veins when the footsteps fall, if it's in another room I can feel it in my room—even from my bed. I wish I at least would remember to turn on the lights. I never do. And now it's so dark and scary.

I'm whispering, can you hear me? He's here—I see his feet under the door. Oh no. I'm so shaky.

Door's opening. Yaaawnnnn.

Shh.

—Denniissss.

—Daddy, go back.

(I always say 'Daddy go back' at first, but it never works. There's a little bit of silence, but I can hear him breathing over me.)

—Denniiisssssss . . .

—Go back, Dad. Please. (I whisper this so low that I doubt he can hear me. I'm more crying than talking.)

—Don't wake your mother, Denny. Do you know why I'm here?

(I nod slowly, my head rubbing tears on my pillow. My dad looks so tall over my bed, like a dark hungry giant or something like that.)

—Because . . . (I start saying like usual) because this isn't really you, right daddy?"

—Right, Denny. This isn't your daddy anymore. It's the devil. And you know why I'm here so late, right baby? Right, Denny?

(I'm trying not to cry because then you can't hear his voice on my recorder. I got this toy on my birthday. It's really neat but it wasn't a lot of money or anything. So I can't cry too loud because then you know you can't hear my dad.)

—Tell me why I'm here, Dennis. (My dad whispered this, but he sounded mad about it.)

—Because you're hungry and you wanna eat me. (Still crying, my voice must sound like I have a million hiccups every second.)

—Mmmmmm . . . that's juuuuust right, Denny Denny. I wanna eat you up. Will you let me this time?

—Please, Dad. Just go back to sleep.

—No way, Jose. Not while I'm so hungry.

(I'm so scared that I feel pee starts wetting me down there like the hose outside in the yard. It's hot and makes me feel like rolling around screaming.)

—Ung! Daddy I peed! (I cry in a loud whisper.)

—You sick boy! All the more reason to eat you up and make you disappear. You better beg, boy.

—Please, please, pleaseee. I want to sleep. Please don't eat me. Please stop, Daddy. I don't want to tell Mommy for real.

—We know you won't do that. And plus, Mommy won't believe you, Dennis.

—I will. And she will because I'm recording this time. So please leave, okay?

(There's more silence, but I can hear him breathing louder, and deeper, and slower. And shakier. He's really really mad now!)

—Where's the recorder? (His voice sounds too normal now, like he's asking on the weekend mornings for coffee or the newspaper.)

—You won't find it. (I say.)

(Silence.)

—Dennis, where's the recorder?

—No.

—Dennis.

—No, Dad. No, devil. Whatever you are, go away and I won't tell my mom on you.

(Outta nowhere, he grabs my arm and yanks it so hard that my neck almost breaks in half. I'm swinging over my bed like a monkey, and my arm hurts a lot. My arm feels like it's twisted around and bended like string cheese.)

—Oowwww (I cry.)

—Okay, Dennis. (He says.) But getttt ready for tomorrow. Th—think hard and get ready, you little shit. I'm gonna start with these little chicken-bone arms of yours. I'll snap them off like wings and eat the skin off like a fucking shish kabob, you hear me boy?

(He drops me on the bed. I bounce. I'm crying so hard that I can't breathe good. Crying so so hard.)

My dad—the devil—leaves the room like a demon ghost.

I keep crying and don't sleep that night till the light eats the shadows for breakfast, through the window, when the sun comes up.

◖

THE NEXT MORNING is Saturday—lucky me—so I get to sleep more than normal. Not super long though, cause my mom comes in a little later and wakes me up. I get scared at first.

"Morning, baby, time to get up," she says, smiling over me.

I twist my blankets over my head. "Not yet."

"Oh," she says. "And what am I supposed to say to your breakfast then, Dennis? 'Sorry, but Dennis is too lazy to come down?' "

I make a sound like a train stopping, because I'm sleepy and I feel a little crazy inside. I hope my mom notices and leaves me alone.

"I'll be waiting downstairs," she says. "Please don't make me come back up here, Dennis."

When she's gone, I turn again in my bed. I look at the top of the room, where the fan is spinning. Each time it turns, it makes a tick that drives me crazy.

Tick-tick-tick, it goes. Tick, tick. Like it's laughing about a secret to the other wings on the fan. They're laughing together. Saying little Dennis has got a devil for a dad. Tick, tick.

I can't believe that it's taken this long to notice the bruise on my arm. Some parts are black and a dirty brownish-blue. It hurts to move it, but I'm glad it's not broken. That would be too hard to hide from my mom. This might be hard to hide too though, since I'm wearing a short sleeve shirt.

I move to my drawer and get a big white long sleeve shirt. It was a shirt we got for free at basketball camp. Not for winning or anything, just for going.

I get my recorder. I listen to the tape—I can hear the words fine, but not very good. It's good enough though.

I hide my recorder behind my bed. That way my dad can't find it. I looked on the internet to look for people who walk around at night when they should be sleeping —it's called sleepwalking. That makes sense, because he's walking but it's not really him. It's the devil.

I go downstairs. I'm especially scared because it's the weekend and my dad will be home. I mean, this is my good dad. Not the devil. So I guess it's different. But it takes me some time in the day like the weekend to re-member that my daddy is not always scary. Now he's the best dad ever—he'll play baseball or football with me even sometimes if I don't ask him.

"Hi, sweetheart," my mom says as I jump up on the seat for breakfast. "Tell me if it's cold and I'll heat it up for you."

I hold my hand on top of the food and feel it a little. "Nope," I say. "It's okay."

Scrambled eggs with bacon and sausage chopped up inside and cheese on top. My favorite. I know my mom always makes this for me on the weekend. That's the main reason why I love the weekend.

I start eating. Even though I barely slept last night, this food makes me feel happy and awake.

I chew fast, like if I haven't had food in days. Really I'm only feeling really hungry because I was awake most of the night, and when I'm awake long, my stomach seems to be awake with me. It growls and coughs and barks like a dog, and it makes a sucking noise like it's sucking whatever is in my stomach to eat instead of food. When I'm done, I burp and push my plate a little.

"Dennis," my mom says from the sink without looking at me. She is washing dishes already. She only says my name, but I know that by the way she said it she means a lot more. The way she says 'Dennis' when she's mad is stuffed with a lot of other meanings. So I know she doesn't like when I burp. I say low that I'm sorry and hop off the big chair.

As I'm leaving the kitchen, I can hear the heavy burble-burble of the water from the sink, and it almost sounds like the sink is burping too.

Then I see my daddy. Before I get to the stairs, he's stepping down the steps, and they make noises like cats crying and elephants walking on wood. When Dad sees me, his face turns happy.

"Hey, Sport!" he says smiling, and rubs my hair as he passes by.

I smile but only for him. I don't have the feeling to smile for myself. To smile for real. I go upstairs and he goes to the kitchen. When I get back to my room, I think about the recorder again. Should I show my dad? I know I recorded it for that, to show him or my mom, but now I'm scared. What if when I show it my dad turns into the devil again? What if when he hears the recording he gets so mad at me for it that he calls up the devil like a rich boy calling his rich daddy to fight for him? Then me and my mommy will be in trouble.

No, maybe I shouldn't say anything.

IT'S TOMORROW ALREADY. Sunday morning. Me and my mom are going to church. My daddy doesn't like to go. Probably because the devil lives inside him. Instead he stays home and watches football on the television. I don't like football, but Daddy says when I'm older I will like it. I think maybe I will, since I'm my dad's son. His breath always smells like beer when he says this close to me though.

Sometimes (today she did it too) my mommy will tell my dad to clean up the house while we're gone for church. She says to him "You need to put in your part" or something like "Your office and Denny's room are always a mess." That's true, my room is always a mess, but not messier than my dad's office. Sometimes Dad cleans like she wants, just to make her happy.

Today at church, Pastor Derrik is talking about loving your family at all times—even when they hurt you or disappoint you. Pastor Derrik isn't the grown-ups pastor, he's the one for kids like me. Our church is close to our house, and the kids section is behind it in a different building. It looks a little bit like a farm here, but I like it. Sometimes they let the kids paint on the walls stuff about God and Jesus, or other Bible people. I've done it once—I drew a picture of Moses opening the Red Sea with his stick. I think it's called a staff. I drew it right by the door. Pastor Derrik smiled and said to me, "Wow Denny! That's a pretty painting." I smiled back and said,

"I don't like it, but thanks." He laughed and gave me candy.

As the pastor talks about love, I think about my dad. I'm confused because I love him but I'm afraid of him, too. Is that normal with love? Should loving my dad and being scared of him live in the same box? I would ask Pastor Derrik but he always looks busy. He's a very talkative person, even though he's kind of old and going bald.

When church is finished, my mom is waiting outside the kids' building with her pretty blue dress. She's wearing a nice hat too that covers the sun light.

"Over here, Dennis!" she says, waving and smiling.

I nod at her while I walk, because I don't like when she says my name out loud like that. It's just the other kids sometimes giggle at me and it makes me mad. I pass her by and she already knows not to bother me. We get in the car and she starts driving home.

"What did Pastor Derrik talk about?" she asked. She always asks this.

"Oh like nothing," I say. "Just like about love and God's love and stuff."

I can see her smiling even though she's looking to the front. "Good. That's good, Denny. Did you like it?"

It's always the same talk we have. I'm looking outside the window at the trees and dogs and people and cars move by me like changing dreams.

"Uh-huh," I say barely.

We get to my house, and Mom opens the door for me even though I can open it myself. I move out of the car and wait for her by the front door of the house while she gets her purse and things from the car. Then she opens the front door and we go inside.

"We're home," my mom says loud, putting her purse on the table and kicking off her tall church shoes. I don't hear the television. Dad isn't watching TV.

My heart stops for a moment.

"Oh honey, you cleaned!" my mom says in a happy voice. The dishes are all done and the floor smells like wet pines.

But my dad doesn't answer. Instead, after a little while, we see him walk slowly down the stairs. His face is whiter than normal. He looks up at us. He looks like the devil again and I get scared. I freeze up.

"Hi honey, nice job!" my mom says.

"Hey," my dad says. He's holding something behind his back.

My mom says, "I'm going upstairs to change. Is the game over?" She means the football game, but my dad doesn't answer. His face is serious.

When my mom is gone upstairs, my dad comes slowly closer to me and I get really scared. I feel like I'm going to faint.

But he doesn't turn to the devil. No—instead, he looks like he's going to cry. And like he was crying before we came home. His mouth starts shaking. He moves his hands from behind his back.

He's holding the tape from my recorder.

"Denny," he says, starting to cry and holding up the tape. "What is this, baby?"

MY DAD TOLD ME that we were going to go for a ride in the car to talk about my recorder and the tape he found. He heard the whole thing while me and Mom were at church. He found it while he was helping clean my room. I should've thought about that but I was too scared to think right. This was not how I wanted my daddy to figure out that he was the devil at night.

We went into my dad's small pick-up truck—my dad called it small once, but to me it's really big and I have to hold the open door to help me jump inside the front seat. The white truck rolled back so fast into the street that I didn't have time to even put my seatbelt the right way. It tapped and tapped with the metal like two swords fighting each other, until the click made it nice and tight. It took long because my dad was jerking the truck to go in different streets. Fast.

Once we get to the back ways of the streets, behind the houses, my dad starts driving slower. I feel my heart beat so hard that the seat belt jumps a little with each beat. I can see the lake that's behind the many houses. The water is soft and calm. It reminds me of the top lid of the jack-in-the-box that one of my friends from school has. His name is Jerry and he got it as a gift from his grandma for Christmas. It's pretty cool. You turn the bar over and over and eventually—wham! Jack comes out of the box. I imagine that the lake is the top part of the box, the lid, and the more my dad drives around the lake, eventually the lid of water will pop open like a volcano and Jack (or something) will pop out. Maybe a big sea monster.

"Dennis—" my dad says, bringing me back to the car and out of the lake in my head. "Was that really me in the tape?" His voice was starting to change in the end of his words, and he glances at me with a sad face.

"What do you mean?" I say.

"I mean," he says, then I see his shoulders fall a little. "How long has this been happening?"

I think about it, playing with my fingers. "For—as long as I can remember."

The car keeps moving, but I can see my dad's face turn almost as white as the clouds behind him, and his hands hold the wheel softer. "What?" he says, like if he didn't hear me. But I'm pretty sure he did cause I said it loud and clear.

"How?" he says. "How-how-how—?" His eyes search the sky like if there's an answer up there.

"I checked online," I say, hopeful. "It's called sleep-walking."

My dad makes a sound like he's laughing in his head. I think he's going crazy.

"Sleep—" he says, then whispers, "*walking.*"

I'm getting scared so I play with my hands again.

"Your mother doesn't know," he says, but since it sounds like it could be a question, I shake my head.

He breathes out slowly and his body shakes some more. "This is not normal, okay Denny? Whatever I've said to you—whatever I've done, it's not a normal thing. Daddies don't do those things— I'm going to take care of this, Denny. I promise you that. I'll go see a doctor and I'll make sure I get better. This will never happen again."

I feel so much better now that my dad said that. Like all the secrets that I've had to keep my whole life are all over the floor like playing cards that face up. I smile and look at him—the part of my dad that is not a devil.

"Denny?" he says, turning back to drive back in the way of our house.

"Yes?" I say.

"Why didn't you tell me sooner?"

I think again. "I don't know," I say, because I can't think normal right now.

"Denny, don't tell your mother. Please. For me. Can you do that?"

Maybe not all the playing cards are face-up. I look at the window. "Yes, Daddy."

I don't see him nod, but I can tell that he does. "And Denny?"

"Yes?"

"Why didn't you start locking your door?"

I know the answer to this one. "Because," I say, happy that I have an answer for him. "You said if I did you were gonna break through the door and eat me for sure."

◖

SO I PROMISED my dad not to tell my mom. He had to stop the truck a little before our house, because he started crying and hugging me when I told him what he said to me. I don't know why he was crying. I think maybe hearing it from me made him extra sad or something. I cried too, because seeing your dad cry is like something that sticks to you. It starts to make you feel melty inside like you're not only gonna cry from your eyes, but maybe from your cheeks and hairs, too. And a sad, tingly feeling, too. He's never cried like that in front of me, and it made me so sad. I hope I never see him that way again.

It's 2:00 a.m. now. My dad told me to lock my door. He told me too that he was going to lock his door. That would make it extra safe and extra hard to get to my room when the devil turns on the light inside him. It's like in fifteen minutes that he'll be up again.

I'm in my bed, with my hands on my stomach and looking at the fan again. It looks like a different monster in the night, like it's mixing the darkness until it gets hard the way my mom mixes the batter to make pancakes. I can feel it breathing too. Every few seconds I feel a little huff of cold air hit my arm, and I know it's the fan. It is a monster. It is alive. And it is watching me.

My fingers move on my stomach fast because I'm scared. I can feel the last ten minutes until 2:15 buzzing and burning like a dragonfly hitting the zapper again and again. Soon. Soon, my brain says. The breath of the fan is saying it too, while mixing the darkness like muddy pancakes—Soon. Pause. Soon. Pause. Soon. Pause. Soon.

Just when I'm about to fall asleep (I lost track of the time a few minutes ago) I hear something go *thump!* on the floor, in the other room. My heart falls like something out of space, and I sit up in my bed, holding the covers to my mouth. I want to scream. I've never wanted to scream this much. This hard. This loud. I want to scream till the neighbors hear. I want to cry until I can hide in the water. But I don't. I just sit there, listening to slow, coming footfalls. And the sound—of something dragging.

This is different, my brain screams at me. The devil knows you tried to get him in trouble. You tried to get him found out! And now he's going to eat you like— like—

A fucking shish kabob, I almost say aloud. But I can't talk. I'm too scared.

I look across the room, over to where my writing desk is. That's where I do my homework sometimes. There's a telephone. I can—

Before I think it, I run over to the desk, jumping off my bed, and grab the phone in the dark. The cold plastic feels more real in the dark.

I know my door is locked, so it might—I hope—take longer for my dad to get in. I run over to the window to get that blue moonlight on me, so that I can see the numbers I'm dialing. Only three. 9-1-1.

I'm happy that they are easy numbers to remember, because right now I can't think very good about anything important. I only think about calling the police tonight because I feel like it's what my daddy—my real daddy, now that he knows—would want me to do.

A lady picks up fast on the phone. "Nine one one— where is your emergency?"

"Hello?" I say with a shaky voice, and I realize I'm sweating.

"Yes, little boy? What's wrong?" The lady on the phone sounds like she's worried, so I feel better a little.

"My dad—is—" I start.

"Do you know your address? What's your address?"

I try to remember my address. I can't think right though because I can hear my dad already pounding at my door.

"My—" I say, thinking between each loud bang of the door. "It's—2114 South—" BANG! "Orange Street—" BANG! "Oh please come!" I cry. "My dad is trying to kill me!"

"The police are on their way, young man. Are you somewhere safe?"

I'm crying harder than I've ever cried in my life. The type of cry that screams from your belly and makes you feel like throwing up because your stomach is shaking so much. "No! I'm not safe!"

Then I hear, from behind the door of my room. "I have a surprise for you, Denny!"

"Go away!" I scream, but it sounds more like a cat falling down the stairs.

"Little boy, I need you to stay on the phone with me, and I need you to find a place to hide," the police lady says, sounding really scared for me.

I look at the closet. I can maybe hide there. Or—or I can maybe jump out the window. Yes! I put down the phone for a second and start to push up the window. But I can't. The cold glass slips on my sweaty hands. I turn to my desk and grab my school scissors. They're not very sharp, but maybe I can use them to give the window and extra push. I try, placing the scissors under the clasp and pushing with every strength I have. It still won't budge. Then, from behind me, I hear a loud crack!-bang!-crash! and throw my head around my shoulders.

My dad—no, he's not even human, he's the Devil of devils—is standing at the door, holding something through his arms. I can hear the police lady saying something on the phone, but the phone is still by the window, and right now, in her faraway electric, static voice, she sounds like no help to me at all.

"Surprise," the devil says, just a tall shadow at my door.

Then he drops the body of my mom on the floor.

◖

I KNEW ALREADY that I'll never forget the sound her legs made when the back part of her feet hit the floor. It was like a normal sound, too normal, like when she would bring home groceries and drop the bag of fruits on the floor. So dead. So fast and empty.

Thud.

My dad walked in front of her. Then I saw his face, melted inside the dark like wax, a moving shadow from the spinning fan rolling over his face. And he was smiling. Not a big smile—just enough to call it one.

"Oh Dennis—" he said. "You really fucked it up this time, buddy."

I hated to hear him say bad words. Because when he said them it meant that, from now on, I would hear him in my head say those words whenever I thought about it. They stuck more than normal words.

I couldn't talk. I tried to say sorry or please or something, but my mouth was so dry that I had to lick the roof of my mouth just to breathe right. In the dark, I looked over at the phone by the window. I still heard the lady talking, but she might as well be just a voice in my head, because she couldn't really help me now. Before I could think about picking up the phone again—maybe just to throw it at my dad—he came up quickly and snatched it.

"What, what—" he said, wagging his head. "You're just being naughty after naughty after naughty, aren't you?"

I couldn't help looking back at my mom now. She could just be another part of furniture in the house, she looked so dead. My heart was a torpedo of fire-beats in me. It made my skin as cold as my mom's dead skin was probably, and my veins felt like they were chugging my blood slowly and coldly through them like cars stuck in snow traffic.

I tried to talk again. My lips tried out different words, words that my mind was screaming, but they never got farther than the back of my tongue. I thought I might choke on them.

The devil smiled and flung the phone across the room. It broke in a million cold plastic pieces that were swallowed by the dark. "You don't need to say anything,

Dennis. Your actions have spoken for you already. Do you know what I mean?"

I tried to swallow but only coughed, and tired tears fell out real sloppy.

"You—" I say. "You promised me you—"

"Devil doesn't make promises, Denny. I just take what I want. Like I took your Mommy. I just—" He moves his hands and grabs his neck, sticking his tongue out, to pretend he's choking himself. He chuckles. "Oh Dennis, you should have seen her eyes. Bigger than baseballs, they were. And so—full of confusion. I think maybe she was having a good dream before I—" he laughed. "Well that didn't last long, now did it? Dennis, you know what I want more than anything in the whole wide world? You know, don't you?"

I'm breathing heavy, and I feel like I'm going to faint.

"Say it!" he screams, his eyes pressed shut. "Say it! Say it!"

"You—"

"Say it!"

"You want to—"

"Say it!"

"—eat—"

"Yeah, bitch—say it! Say it!"

I jump forward when he's close enough and stick the scissors into his stomach. It feels gooey and soft, like I'm sticking a knife in a tub of cold butter. Since he's wearing a shirt, I can tell that the scissors don't go all the way in, but it's enough that my dad screams and shoves me against the window. When I bump it, I can hear something outside. Two police cars—no, three—race to the driveway. One almost hits my dad's truck, off by like an inch. The tires scratch the floor and I think I see smoke fly.

I turn back to see my dad, his eyes still closed, and he's seeing over me.

"Oh, Dennis—you didn't," he says, still holding his stomach where I put the scissors. But he's almost laughing as he says this, like if he can't believe how stupid I am for trying to get help. Somewhere downstairs, I hear yelling. I didn't hear the police break the door, but I know they're in now.

I'm stuck by the window, with my dad in front of me, and the closet behind to the right. I know I can't reach it without the devil snatching me first.

"Looks like we've got company," he says. But as he says that, he's looking down at the blood all sticky from his stomach that's starting to come out. I see him swish around in his eyes like he's dizzy and he has to hold the lamp by the window to stay up standing up. I take this chance to run over to the closet where I hide.

"Freeze!" I hear the policeman say from the hall. "Come out with your hands up, hands up!"

I hear a loud thump as my dad—or the whatever he is!—falls down on the floor. The lamp comes down with him and smashes a thousand bits. By this time I'm in the closet already. And I hear the policemen come in fast, yelling and stepping around fast. They say some words, first loud, then whispering, like: "Go, go. That's him! He's down." They move around the room some more, dropping things and I hear some of my toys break.

In my closet, there are like little windows to see through. Little skinny bars—*slits*—that show, barely, the room outside. I look through them, but I can't see much. just shadows crossing by different shadows. Where's my dad?

I'm sitting shaking in the black closet, my butt on some old sneakers and my pants and t-shirts hanging over my face like those plastic flaps in a carwash.

"I found something," one of the policemen say.

"What is it?" says another.

"I don't know. Press play," a third says.

It's my recorder. They found it. I push my head close to the door, listening hard.

The recorder starts.

"I don't know what to do," the voice says. But it's not my voice. *"My son Dennis . . . he's murdered my wife."*

My heart feels like it stopped. What was this recording? How did he . . .

"God . . . if . . . what can I do? If you're listening to this, then something drastic has happened. Either we've gone into hiding, or my son and I are dead. I can't imagine what horrible life could await him here if people found out. A life as a child murderer. And a life without his mother. He'd be better off dead with his parents. Well . . . my son is somewhere in his room now. I don't think he even knows what's happened. He just came in about an hour ago and started yelling something about the Devil being in us. He's not right in the head. God . . . God . . . . I had to tell somebody, but I can't tell the police. I just can't." He starts crying hard. *"He's my son! My God. My God! Christ, what do I do? He's not a bad boy. He's not. But how could something like this—I don't know. It doesn't make sense.*

It just—Jesus . . . he's back! Dennis . . . Denny, baby, put down the scissors. Please baby, Denny put that down. Don't make Daddy take . . . Dammit! You stabbed me!" There's a static noise that hides the rest and the recorder stops.

I can't breathe. I'm sitting like I'm almost dead in the closet, and I can't breathe or even move. I can hear the police saying some words like they're mad at *me* now! What if they find me here? What if . . . ?

I hear them coming.

"Dennis, open that closet door and come out slowly."

Oh, no. They know I'm here. But I didn't do nothing! I didn't!

"Come out, slowly, Dennis."

It was the Devil! my mind cries.

I'm breathing real heavy and hard. The floor under me is creaking because they're close. I can still hear my Dad—*no, he was never my Dad, never my Dad*—laughing in my head.

"Come out now or you'll *really* be in trouble," the policeman says.

I start to cry hard as they open the closet door.

"It was the Devil!" I weep, throwing the bloody scissors past them. *"The Devil tried to eat me!"*

◖ The Glitch

DANIEL DEAN CIRCLED THE PARKING LOT for nearly five minutes, clutching the steering wheel of his sedan with moist hands, drumming anxiously at the wheel with his index fingers.

"Dammit!" he shouted, his hoarse early morning voice sounding unconvincing in the small interior of his car. "One, God dammit. I'm looking for one damn space!"

Finally, he saw a parking space near the end of the lot. It would mean running farther to get to his interview, but since there were no other available spots in the lot—none that he could find, at least—he twisted his car into the space. He jerked the gear to PARK, and twisted off the key from the ignition in a quick, seemingly rehearsed motion. Almost leaping from his car, he started off through the parking lot in a quick walk. Soon his walk became a jog, then, thinking again that he was almost ten minutes late to his big interview, his jog became a senseless dash. He didn't care if anyone saw him. Better that they chuckle or think whatever they might (although, realistically, they probably wouldn't think much of him at all) than for Daniel to be late. His interviewer, Gwen Russell, made it very clear that if Daniel missed the interview, she wouldn't be able to reschedule. The position was too valuable and too many applicants were in line for the job. He replayed their conversation in his mind as he ran frantically, shaking his head in fear and panic. *No*, he thought. *No, I have to explain myself. I need to make her understand. My alarm didn't wake me. I'm not at fault. I'll put the full blame on my alarm. My fucking alarm. Thanks a lot, you worthless piece of crap.*

He was almost near the end of the parking lot when he noticed another free parking space.

"Really?" he muttered breathlessly. "Are you fucking kidding me?" Didn't matter. There was no help for that now. He pushed down the anger he felt within and continued to jog towards the building. He had to cross the street first. The intersection was usually pretty packed. Fortunately, it was clear today and he forced his tired legs to continue on through the street. He looked both ways and crossed. The sun, he noticed as he went, was hiding behind a gray cloud. The contrast of the light hitting the cloud made the cloud look glorious.

He slowed his pace to a more relaxed walk once he reached the middle of the crossing. He waited for two cars to pass (hurry hurry faster you idiots!) then walked quickly across. He could see the building from a short distance. Almost there. Almost—

Daniel felt a hot pain wrack his body, his face. He froze in terror. He thought someone had punched his nose. Rubbing his stinging face and, he discovered quickly, bleeding nose, he turned sharply.

"What the hell?" he cried, looking around maniacally. "Who—"

But no one was there. He turned back to cross the street and was stopped again by—

What?

He reached his hands out and felt the air in front of him. His hands met something flat and solid, like a wall. An invisible wall.

"What in the hell is this?" he grunted. He slapped the invisible wall that prevented him from crossing the street. "What in God's name is going on?"

He turned just in time to see a car approaching quickly. The car honked its horn and swerved to the left, nearly hitting Daniel.

"Jesus!" he cried, wringing his body against the wall.

"Get off the fucking road!" the man driving called out to him.

Daniel felt the invisible wall behind him again. His mind couldn't fathom what it was.

HE RAN BACK in the direction of his car, looking both ways dizzily until he reached the sidewalk. He felt a surge of relief almost instantly as he realized that, indeed, he was able to reach the sidewalk and avoid the sudden wave of traffic.

He leaned forward weakly and rested his hands on his knees.

Must be— he thought for a while. *Must be some glass panel they put there to block the way*, he thought stupidly. *Sure, that's it, you moron. A glass panel. Why not? That makes sense. Moron.*

"Oh shut up," he muttered to himself. "Then what is it?" He absently dabbed a finger across his nostril and drew cold blood. It wasn't much, but enough to worry him.

The interview, he thought again with weighing dread. *No way I'll be excused now. I'll have to call in and say there was a family emergency. My mother died.* She'd been dead three years anyway, so the usual fear of jinxing the situation wasn't an issue. Anything. Anything to remedy the situation.

He reached for his phone. His phone was dead.

"What the—" Then he remembered that he'd forgotten to charge it the night before. "Shit," he muttered.

He started for the other side of the block with his head lowered. Just as suddenly, he felt a ring of pain shoot across his forehead.

No. The realization hurt more than the physical pain. Impossible. No, no it's not possible.

He reached up and felt the wall. The wall that wasn't visibly there. He looked around. A man was crossing the street and he could feel the stranger's eyes hovering over him.

"There's something here," Daniel said, trying not to panic. "You feel it?"

The man shook his head uncomfortably and continued walking. *He thinks I'm crazy*, Daniel realized.

He wiped blood from his nose, and walked to the left and right of him. To the right, another invisible wall blocked his way almost immediately (this time he had the sense to raise his arms and protect himself against the contact of the wall). To his left, he was able to walk a short distance—maybe thirty feet—before the wall came into existence. For a while, he'd gotten excited, thinking that the wall hadn't manifested from this angle. But when he felt it finally, his shoulders slumped and he let out a whimper.

Tears formed in his eyes. "Is this *some kind of joke?*" he shouted.

The people around him who'd been watching this man in a suit reach his arms out and press his palms against an invisible wall like a mime, pretended to ignore him. The ones who crossed the street he was on did so without trouble, passing through the wall that Daniel couldn't penetrate. He couldn't say anything because they wouldn't believe him anyway. This terrified him more. He started to feel the sweat beat down on him and looked quizzically at his suit.

"Jesus," he said, looking at the sleeves of his suit like handcuffs. He stripped the suit off and walked over to the shade beneath the bridge.

He wasn't crying anymore. That ended quickly, he was proud to notice. *Okay*, he thought. *I can keep my cool here. I can work this out. There's an explanation for this.* He suddenly got the idea to trace the entire block that surrounded him. Maybe there was some kind of opening. Or a trail, like a maze. He straightened up with a frail thread of hope and began with the corner he was near, right by the parking lot and under the bridge. He felt the wall with his fingers (*What is it?* he thought—it felt like glass but the resemblance ended there) and started to walk in a straight line, watching out for traffic. Some of the cars that did pass, seeing this odd man walking zombified with his hand reaching out for something invisible, honked their horns at him. He ignored them. The wall felt smooth—*like glass*, he thought again. He reached the other side of the street, then turned as the wall directed him. In the end, he made it back to his starting point, and there were no openings. It was a perfect rectangle. He leaned his body on the wall, still caught in stupefied amazement.

The sun was getting hotter now; every cell of his body seemed to be buzzing with intense heat, releasing sweat from more pores than he thought he had.

"Mother—" he muttered, holding out the second part of that profane phrase. He wore a white sweaty dress shirt. *Cotton*, he thought vaguely. He unbuttoned the two top buttons and rolled up his sleeves. Then, grunting in frustration, he untucked his shirt.

He realized he had walked under the bridge now. That was in the same vicinity of the rectangular wall that entrapped him.

Trapped, he thought. Until now, for some reason, it hadn't seemed real. In the back of his mind, this had been some kind of prank. A practical joke. Soon there'd be a man in a funny suit stepping out from behind the bridge, announcing that Daniel Dean had been fooled, pointing out the hidden cameras here—and there—and there.

But then something innate in him reacted. It happened so suddenly that he found himself moving before his brain could react. He ran across the street—a car nearly hit him again—and jumped into the invisible wall. His body shuddered and he landed on the ground. His head felt hot with different emotions, all negative, as he began to pound his fists on the wall.

"Open up!" he yelled. "This isn't funny, Goddamit! Don't you know I lost an interview because of you?! I was gonna make a good living!"

Cars continued to honk as they passed him, slowing down, getting a better look at this crazy man. Daniel gave them the finger.

◖

AN HOUR LATER, he began to panic completely. He felt cold inside, despite the intensifying heat.

"Excuse me," he said to a woman in her thirties who was headed for the bus stop. She stopped hesitantly and waited. "This is going to sound crazy," he said. "But—but I seem to be stuck here."

"Stuck?"

"There's—there's some sort of wall here," he said, realizing even as he spoke that she would not believe him.

The lady looked at him as if he were abstract painting in a museum, then she shook her head and continued walking off to the bus bench, passing the impenetrable wall that he couldn't seem to cross. Daniel stood dumbfounded, feeling a new reserved wave of heat bubble hotly against his already-sweating body.

"Shit!" he cried, his body racking uncontrollably.

His phone was dead, so he asked another man passing by to call 911. He couldn't call any of his friends (although he didn't have many) because he didn't know any of their numbers by memory. And he didn't have any immediate family members. Both his parents were dead, he was an only child, and all his relatives lived in California, where he lived. He was only in Miami for his chance at the big interview, which was shot to hell now. Three hundred thousand dollars. That was the salary they were offering.

His relatives, none of which were very close to him, would worry enough to track him down all the way from the other side of the country. He hadn't told anyone about his trip, because he didn't want the pressure on him. A foolish idea, he thought in retrospect. *Oh shut up!* he told himself. *How was I supposed to know something like this could happen?*

He decided 911 was his best option.

"My phone is dead," he explained to the man. "And I think I'm having a heart attack." He pressed his hands against his chest and feigned convulsions. "Please, *please.*"

The man turned white and reached for his phone faster than Daniel had expected. In a moment, he had the police on the line. "A man is having a heart attack." The man, who wore a black jacket that was way too hot for this weather and donned a black fedora, soon hung up and said, "They're on their way. How's your heart?"

Daniel nodded, swallowing dryly for dramatic effect. "It seems to be holding out."

When they arrive, Daniel thought, *I can definitely convince them to help me.*

THE AMBULANCE ARRIVED in five minutes. Daniel heard it from a distance, beyond the draw bridge, then saw the red top of the truck with its flashing lights as it climbed over the draw bridge like a whale emerging from the ocean. He sat neatly on the sidewalk, and although he'd said it was unnecessary, the man in the black fedora had insisted on staying with him. He sat there beside him, offering a slight smile as a sort of soothing anesthetic, occasionally asking Daniel how he felt.

"A little better," he kept saying. It felt oddly refreshing to know that there were some kind people out there in the world. He wasn't sure if he would do the same for someone else. The world had made him too numb to the sensitivity of others, let alone strangers. The man didn't even look hot in his jacket and hat, though Daniel did note the small beads of sweat planted on his face like land mines.

The ambulance parked half on the right lane of the street and half on the sidewalk. Two uniformed men came out and while one retrieved a stretcher in the rear of the truck, the other went straight for Daniel.

"It's this man," the man in the hat said to the medic. The medic crouched down to Daniel's level.

"How do you feel?" he asked. For some reason, Daniel felt humiliated. The man who'd been waiting with him suddenly started off, wishing Dan good luck.

"My heart feels funny," Daniel said. "Can you take me to the hospital?"

The other man—the one who'd gotten the stretcher—came forth and suddenly grabbed Dan's arm. He held it out and the medic attached some cables with sticky ends to his arm.

"Just take me—" Daniel started, then stopped himself.

After a minute, the medic said, "You're fine. Nothing seems to be wrong."

"Well, something is wrong. I know it. I can feel it."

"Have you been taking any medication? Any—drugs?"

Daniel shot his head back. "No! Christ, I was on my way to a job interview. I'm not on drugs!"

"All right," the medic said. "We can take you to the hospital if you'd like."

Daniel nodded. "Please."

They helped him up and he said the stretcher was unnecessary. He'd almost forgotten the wall was there—until it hit him. He stopped cold.

The medics turned and looked at him strangely. "Do you feel it again?"

"Yes," Daniel said, tears in his eyes. But he meant that he felt the wall, not a heart attack.

The medics rushed over to him. "Let's get you in the truck."

Daniel felt his body go limp, but the medics caught him and started to walk him towards the truck. Then they both grunted and turned as Daniel stopped. "Come on, man," one of them said. "Let's go." He tugged again but Daniel was stuck behind the wall.

"Jesus, this guy's strong. You gotta let us take you," the other medic said. He tugged again. Daniel looked at them in a daze of weariness, a glaze of tears shielding his vision.

"It's not letting me," he said. "I can't go."

The medic's eyes grew sharp, as if they suspected he might be having another heart attack.

"You feel it again?" the one asked.

Daniel nodded and moved to sit on the sidewalk again. They moved to him and checked his heart again. "Your heart still checks out fine," one of them said. "You sure you aren't on any medication? Any history of anxiety and panic attacks?"

Daniel stayed quiet, watching the slow traffic move behind the two uniformed men. The air felt still and foreign, the noise of the cars sounded patronizing. Daniel felt a pinch of anger coat his heart and he grunted.

The men stood straight up after checking his heart. They looked like towering skyscrapers shadowed by the sun. "Look," one of them said, his tired hands on his hips. "We can't force you to come with us. You seem okay to us. Just try to relax and you should be fine. Get yourself some water, you look dehydrated." They looked at each other and then back at Daniel. "You need anything else?"

Daniel stayed quiet. Then after a moment, the two paramedics left in their truck. They drove without their sirens, no emergency now.

◖

HE MUST HAVE CRIED for an hour, or at least long enough for the sun to move a noticeable distance in the sky, casting different tones of light. The heat was more intense now. Daniel was sitting shirtless, sweating, feeling sunburned and feverish. He was moaning without knowing it, his body shifting and lolling from side to side. He had completely lost perception of time and the people around him. As far as he was concerned, they were equally unimportant as the clouds drifting slowly across the sky. Some of them pretended not to notice him; others either pursed their lips in pity or dropped a dollar or some coins beside him. *My grand fortune*, he thought once. *Who needs a fancy job when you have this?*

"Hey, bro, can I buy you a hotdog?"

Daniel turned towards a man who was hovering over him. The sun was hiding behind the man's head which veiled his face with blotchy shadows.

Daniel hadn't realized how hungry he was. "Yes," he said quickly. "Please, yes."

The man nodded, his hands on his hips. He wore a white t-shirt that said A Church For Sinners Only. Daniel couldn't decide if that was the actual name of the church or just an ironic phrase.

"You got it, buddy. Wanna come along?" The man pointed to the hotdog stand on the other street, but Daniel shook his head. "I—I can't uh—" he stuttered, because he didn't want to appear crazy to the man. A vain hope, he realized. "Can—can you bring it to me instead?"

The church man nodded and combed his hair back with his pudgy fingers. The man started off leisurely, whistling softly. In a few minutes, he was back with a hotdog and a bottle of water.

"Here ya go, friend," he said, a thin film of sweat carpeted on his forehead.

Daniel had forgotten to ask for water, the most important thing. Thank God this man had thought of it for him.

"Thank you so much," Daniel said, smiling for the first time in a while.

The man nodded and smiled in return. "So what's your story, man. You homeless?"

Daniel felt embarrassed by the assumption, by the fact that he looked homeless enough for someone to suggest that so casually. Him, homeless. He owned a two-story house in LA for Christ's sake.

"It's a long story," he said.

The man shrugged and then sat down beside him. "Listen—I'll believe whatever story you tell me. You don't look like a bad guy. I just don't picture you a victim of drug abuse."

Cars passed by obliviously. Daniel looked at the shirt again. A Church For Sinners Only. Maybe this Jesus Freak was the best person to tell his crazy story to.

"I came here for a job interview," he started, his cheeks blushing. "Next thing I knew, I was stuck on this street."

"Stuck?" The man asked.

"Yes," he said. "That's what I mean exactly. Some kind of invisible wall is keeping me here."

Even as he spoke, Daniel could see the transformation in the man's face. The man's eyes went from patient sympathy to uncomfortable anxiety. He kept looking around as Daniel spoke. Daniel's words seemed to fall flatter as he realized he was losing the man's trust and attention.

Suddenly, Daniel stopped himself and grunted. "Aren't you a man of faith? Don't you believe in forces outside of human control? Demons? The devil? A spiritual realm? This is the same thing! I can't explain it, but it's real!"

Daniel didn't quite believe in all that stuff himself, but he hoped that the man did.

The man was starting to stand up. He seemed afraid. "I believe in—certain things, sure. But—" he was wagging his head, "—this is different. The Bible doesn't talk about this."

Oh great, Dan thought. *It's not in the Bible*. What difference did that make? It was happening to him, wasn't it? Should he run it through the Bible to make sure? He grunted and lowered his head.

"All right," he said as the man started to back away. "Thanks for the food and water."

IT WAS NEARING five o'clock. Daniel was lying against the pavement, under the bridge, listening to the loud roar bouncing off the walls of the underpass as cars sped by. The sound was making him insane. His water bottle was empty, and he'd tossed the aluminum foil from his hotdog into the garbage can. The can was past the invisible wall, but the foil wrapper went through without a problem.

He had to pee. He was lucky enough to find a long bush behind him and pissed in there. Nobody stopped him. *Soon I'll have to poop, too*, the dreadful thought came. He pushed the thought away.

He moved and walked to the corner of the wall closest to the intersection. He pressed his hands against the invisible wall. What was it? he wondered. He'd thought up theories all day, wondering if maybe it was something alien from another planet, or God, or just a glitch in the universe. As if life were a video game with fuck-ups that come from time to time. Rare, but they come. He just happened to be in the wrong spot at the wrong time. And now? Would God, or whoever's in control, fix this glitch? Or would he be stuck here forever? The thought made his bones turn to cold noodles.

Then he noticed a woman coming his way. She was naturally attractive. She'd just exited the building where he was to do his job interview. She had blonde hair pulled up in a bun, and wore a gray suit and held a clipboard and a small leather portfolio. Her glasses were pressed smartly against her face and she wasn't smiling. Her expression was unreadable. She seemed to be in her late thirties, like Daniel. When she was close enough, Daniel saw her name tag.

Gwen.

He felt his heart jump and his face went red. He looked at his suit crumpled on the ground and imagined how sunburned his face looked and how dirty he must have looked. How atrocious he smelled. His hair was a sweaty heap on his head. Gwen. Gwen, dearest Gwen. He knew the name as soon as he read it.

Gwen. The manager who'd scheduled to interview him.

◖

NIGHT HAD FALLEN in the city. One more person had brought Daniel a bottle of water and a burger. He'd gotten some more money without asking for it—pity money for the pitiful man. It was useless, though, since he couldn't leave anywhere to use it, anyway. Instead he planned on asking someone to buy him breakfast with it tomorrow. Tomorrow. The concept was ludicrous and terrifying. A whole day. He'd been trapped here an entire day. He sat leaning against the stop sign pole, smoking a cigarette that someone had given him. He watched the smoke curl and dispatch into the violet sky. He hadn't smoked in years, and even then only did so socially, but he felt comfort from it now. He felt as if he wasn't quite alone.

The cars came more infrequently now, softly humming past the intersection and passing Daniel as if he were a part of the scenery. Maybe he was. Just another piece of litter on the street.

When his cigarette reached its snub end, he tossed it into the street, and a luxurious black car rolled over it carelessly.

THE NEXT DAY, Daniel opened his eyes before the sun had even shown hints of entry in the dark blue clouds. For a questionable second, he turned to the right and was expecting to see his bedroom window, veiled by a thin white curtain. Instead, he saw cars roaming sideways and a black cat standing two feet from his face, gazing at him quizzically. Daniel sat up and wiped the saliva from his chin. Little pebbles from the ground were coated on the saliva like sprinkles. He looked around, depression returning to him in full effect. There were four other homeless men under the bridge, still asleep. They had bags and makeshift mattresses to comfort them. Pillows made of newspapers and wrapping foam.

Daniel hadn't thought about sleeping arrangements that night, he'd been too scared, his thoughts too evasive. He couldn't even remember when he'd fallen asleep, or when the homeless group had come to the underpass. Some of them wiggled and turned in their beds, but ultimately they looked at peace. *How?* Daniel wondered. He couldn't imagine living this way for much longer. And yet, how long had these bums been here? *Bums*—the word tasted foul now. It sounded disrespectful and un-true. They weren't bums. Bum sounded like lazy. Even weak. But these men had very difficult lives, no doubt. Daniel knew that in just a day. *Will this be my life now?* he thought. A chill pricked his spine. *At least those homeless can come and go as they please. They can travel if necessary or desired.* He, on the other hand, was imprisoned within the parameter of this faux wall. Faux, not quite. The wall wasn't fake. It was very much real. He remembered some preacher say once that faith is the evidence of things unseen. *Well, Mr. Preacher Man*, he thought in a mocking voice, *can faith break down these walls? Because it didn't take much faith to build them up in the first place.*

He grunted and stood. *Another day in paradise*, he thought and sighed. *Maybe I should just kill myself.*

"Not yet," he whispered to himself. "Let me try a little longer. If nothing works, sure, I'll consider—that route."

He thought that maybe he could commit some sort of crime to get attention. But which? He didn't want to hurt anybody, just get their attention.

Then the idea came. Indecent exposure. If he got naked in public, the police and maybe even the news will

come. That, he contemplated, should be enough to convince them that the wall is real, when they can't force
me out of it. But that hadn't worked on the paramedics,
a deeper voice reminded him. *No, but it's still worth a
shot.*

Should he wait until the streets got more crowded?
No, why would he? That would only be more embar-
rassing. It would be crowded soon enough, when the
police and the news arrived.

He stood motionless for a while before the soft
traffic, contemplating his arbitrary plan. His hands
clutched the bottom of his dress shirt, which was now
wrinkled with dry sweat and pebbles and dirt. He
unbuttoned his shirt from the bottom up. Even at this he
felt himself beginning to blush. *What am I thinking?* he
thought again. *Is this the way I wanna do this?*

His shirt was off; he flung it to the side. He was afraid
now, standing there shirtless, watching some women
walk by. He gripped his pants—but he just couldn't bring
himself to pull them down. Embarrassment consumed
him. *No,* he thought. *I'll find another way.* He went over to
reach for his shirt, crouched down.

His fingers smashed against the invisible wall.

"Fuck!" he cried. He fell back and held his throbbing
fingers against his chest. The pain sent sharp waves up
his arm. "God dammit! God damn it all! Fuck—*fuck!*"

People were looking at him intently. He stopped a
man.

"Please man," he said. "Can you get my shirt?"

The man regarded Daniel's filthy presence. "Sorry,"
he said, picking up his pace.

Daniel wanted to shout at the man, lash out in anger, but for some reason he restrained himself. Maybe because he saw someone else coming—a lady—and he didn't want to scare her away too.

"Ma'am," he said, and she slowed down hesitantly. "Can you please pick up my shirt? I threw my back."

She stopped over mindlessly and handed him the shirt. Only, the wall was in between them.

"Toss it to me," he said, and she did.

How downright ridiculous he felt.

◖

THREE MORE DAYS had passed. His mind was beginning to lose its rationality. His motives were senseless and capricious. He'd made some homeless friends under the highway. There was Bob, a brown-haired man in his fifties, tight brown skin; Alberto, a Cuban man who was almost in his seventies, too weak to move much so he mostly sat on his black crate and smoked cheap cigars; Leonardo, another Hispanic who was always bitterly scratching his bald head and shouting at rich strangers; and Sammy, a man in his early forties who claimed he'd been falsely convicted of selling drugs four times. They each had their own section under the highway, almost like their imaginary bedroom. During the day, though, they all split up and began their begging.

"No vacation days in this job," Sam had said once, sealing the statement by spitting on the ground near

Daniel's foot. In those three days, the four homeless asked Daniel several times why he never left the block.

"You wouldn't believe me if I told you," Dan had said.

"Ha!" Alberto had coughed in laughter, some tobacco smoke fleeing his mouth. "Wha ju say, I bill-eef!" His Cuban accent was thick and beefy, even for his small, thin figure.

Daniel forced a smile and shrugged. After he told them the story, they each made their own unique facial expression of disbelief.

Bob chuckled. "You're right, you are definitely crazy."

"Never said I was crazy. It's the truth."

Leonardo laughed. "Well if that's the truth, you definitely belong here with us."

That was the end of that conversation. And the homeless helped Daniel get the water and food he needed. He even sent them on errands to get him books to read.

He read a lot that summer.

◖

STUCK, STUCK, he sang in his mind. Stuck like a truck, stuck as fuck. He drummed his fingers against the invisible wall. He'd been trapped so long that he could actually see the walls now. He'd painted its frame in his mind. It was his home. Six months had passed.

One winter night while he was asleep, some kids had spray-painted a box around his home in red. They wrote

"THE PANTOMIME BUM" and "COME ONE, COME ALL!" along the perimeter of the red box.

Kids would come and make faces at Daniel, some would throw trash at him, or run in and steal his books. Sometimes they would moon him, or run in to push him against the invisible wall to see how he'd crash into it. The news came once to do a story on him, but no one believed him or helped him. By that point, he hardly believed himself. This was his life now. He'd accepted it.

"Mommy," a boy said as he crossed the street with his mother. "Give me a dollar for the man."

His mother pulled him aside and whispered harshly. "No, sweetie, don't go near him. He's sick in the head."

◖ On and On

HE STUMBLED FOR two lengthy steps before catching his weight on a traffic post. He stood straight, rigid. Michael Dillon looked to both sides; to his left he saw the traffic of an avenue he cared not the name of, to his right, bushes and distant houses.

He kept on walking. He thought about water and food, the pleasantness they would bring him, but couldn't get himself to stop for some. He felt a trickle of sweat roll down his forehead and dabbed at it absently. And on he walked.

◖

MICHAEL WAS a couple miles off the road, shuffling his tired legs through dirt and rocks. He saw trees ahead, escorting him into a dense forest.

He grunted. His thighs felt like melting lead pipes, and it took everything to keep his legs from buckling under his weight. He bounced off of a crisp, old tree, then fumbled onto another. He almost vomited, but suppressed it. He could feel the acidic soup bubbling up his throat, rising and dipping like lava in a volcano, unable to stifle it.

"My God," he mumbled, shifting his weight and almost falling again. He didn't know why he was even here. He'd left his home last night, at around midnight. He and his wife had endured a full-fledged argument that had lasted almost an hour. He could hardly remember what they had argued about—Beth, his daughter? Perhaps, something related to her. That was usually the case. You work too much, Sarah would often say. What about the kid? She barely knows you exist.

"What an exaggeration!" Michael spat now, his head lolling dizzily from side to side.

He found himself deep in the woods, surrounded by a gang of trees. The sun blinked through the branches haphazardly. *What am I doing?* Michael thought again—and again, he had no reasonable answer. Sarah must be worried sick. He could picture her pacing the room, her hands shaking nervously in her pockets. Hell, she'd probably called the police by now.

Michael fell. He didn't notice he'd fallen until his hands were clenching the dirt with scraped palms, his face inches from the ground.

"Whoa," he muttered on the ground. He rested his weight on his elbows and remained downed on the dirt.

He realized that his knees were scratched up bad too; felt a poisonous sting licking his feeble skin.

He flattened his body on the ground. In less than a minute, his mind retreated to numbing sleep.

MICHAEL GROANED PAINFULLY as he stirred awake. He half expected to find himself at home, in his soft bed. Instead, he awoke to a large rock nestled tautly against his ribs. He didn't even remember the rock being there, but then again, he couldn't remember much at all—except that he had for some reason walked to this spot.

He rose from the ground wearily and stumbled into motion again. He wasn't as hungry or thirsty anymore, but he knew that only put him at more of a risk. He licked his lips; his tongue felt like stale Scotch tape. Michael coughed once and felt a taut pain swell in his chest cavity. He looked at his hands, almost expecting to see blood. There wasn't any. Only specks of hot saliva.

He instinctively reached for his cell phone—he wanted to call Sarah, tell her to come get him; tell her that he was scared and lost—but when he patted his pockets, he found them empty. He'd forgotten that he left his phone at home. Of course he did. *Good*, he thought bitterly. *I don't want to talk to that bitch anyway. Not until she apologizes to me.*

He dazedly looked to the trees for confirmation. They shimmied in agreement.

THE LAST OF the thick trees were behind him now, and Michael stood haplessly before a stream. It must have been at least a quarter of a mile in length.

"I'm not swimming that," he said, his voice dipped in cold fear.

Turn around and go home, he thought for the hundredth time. He wasn't even mad at Sarah anymore. Not for any reason specifically. Why was he here? Why did he have to show his feelings in this way? He was upset—yes. And frustrated. But why couldn't he just go gambling or drinking with his friends? His mind felt submerged in a toxic fog, and he could, for the life of him, peer neither over nor under it.

Turn around and go home, he begged his mind, even as his shoes stepped into the muddy water. Then his knees. Then his waist. All the energy he'd lost falsely returned to him when he felt how terribly freezing the water was. His limbs were almost instantly numbed, and he swam across almost as if watching himself in third-person perspective. The sour water filled his mouth and he swallowed small pools of it. His eyes burned like water forming to ice.

He was halfway across the stream now. He'd drifted a little, but not much. His feet shifted over the slimy stones beneath the water, and he waddled like a toddler to keep his balance. Once he reached the other side, he literally had to crawl out onto the grass. His body shook fitfully, sending spasms of electric pain throughout his entire body.

"I'll die—" he hummed, but a coughing fit overtook him. His entire thought was 'I'll die of pneumonia' but he couldn't manage all the words.

As he contemplated remaining immobile on the ground (immobile save for the endless chills racking his body) beneath the pressing heat of the sun, his arms lifted him to his knees, and his knees aided him to his feet.

From there he continued on walking. Probably dying of pneumonia like he feared, he thought. But that didn't stop him. He wanted so badly to cry and run home.

But his legs stumbled on wearily.

◖

"HO 'UN—HI, MISTER," a young boy said.

He was standing directly over Michael, but he couldn't see the boy because he was lying face down.

The boy poked his ribs with a fishing rod. Michael grunted, craned his neck and propped himself up on his elbows. The sunlight was a pure white sheet enveloping his eyes. Michael had to lie down again. His head throbbed at the sight of the light—a piercing, viperous pain that sent paralyzing signals to his entire body.

"Mister." The boy poked him again, and Michael heard the crunch of grass as he took a step back.

"What?" Michael said, his lips kissing the grass. His lips and mouth and throat were in such a drought that his voice sounded as if it were coming through the fizzy waves of a radio broadcast.

"You're on mu'lawn," the boy said. "Get out 'fore my dad sees."

He could hear the boy walking away; heard the light crunching of grass grow fainter and fainter. When Michael looked up, the boy was gone.

Michael got up and looked around. His body was racked with the scourge of a fever. Michael thought about the stream and frowned. Where the hell was he now? He couldn't even remember walking this far. And he was sick. Very sick. He felt it; he could feel his bones squeaking with weakness, his skin cooked and disease-ridden, the flesh beneath his eyes carrying a concentrated heat that made it hard to see. *I'm dying*, he thought suddenly. The thought was unbidden, but he somehow knew it to be true. He could feel it; death scratching at the doorpost of his body. Every sour, ashy new breath was a charity. His mind could hardly think straight.

He looked down. Without his knowing it, his feet had begun walking again. He began to sob.

"No, no," he cried. "Please take me home."

He was addressing his feet, his legs—as silly as that sounded. It wasn't silly to him at all, though. Not to a man this desperate for his life.

But on he walked; the muscles in his legs felt like chewed-on and spit-out steak. The boy's farm was behind him now, growing smaller by the minute. The path he walked was indirect, looking something like a forest but more like a graveyard—bleak and secluded and packed with dead and dying trees. Michael watched his feet move through a film of runny tears, his mouth catching the salty rivulets like a funnel.

"Don't go that way," he cried again, his voice a broken mishap.

My pride, it's my pride, he cursed in his mind. His brother had warned him. His mother had warned him. His father—God rest his soul—had warned him all of his life. You're the most prideful person I know, they had all said at one time or another. One day, that pride is gonna kill you, his older brother Jeff had said in an argument.

—is gonna kill you, echoed his mind. Now he walked in the forest—probably the third since he left his home . . . when? Two, three days ago? He couldn't even remember. He only knew that he was dying. Of thirst, of hunger, of fatigue, of pneumonia, of diseases he couldn't yet see but could feel. He tried to steer his feet to move left. To move right. To stop. All in vain. All they would do is walk in the pride his mind clung to.

"STOOOOOP!" He yelled, and a bird took flight in the distance.

The sun was coming down. The sky—the part he could see that was not covered by trees—was a dark orange and purple. He looked ahead of himself, saw more forest. He thought about Sarah, and now that memory was more a dream than a reality.

"Then I'll just die," he muttered under his breath. "Fine, if that's what it takes."

Even now, even on the brink of dying, his pride—once again—forbade him to think clearly. A smile turned on his lips, twisted his cheeks. He let out a dry laugh, then coughed. Then he laughed again.

"SARAAAAH!" he cried. "Loook what you made me do! THIS IS ALL YOUR FAULT!"

His pride was being satisfied. He could feel it even over the churning of death inside of him. Felt the pleasure of it. It was like cool water running over his mouth, like the smell of burning steak rushing into his hungry nostrils. It was better than all that. Pride was the vice that satisfied him. And so he walked deeper into the woods holding its hand. Laughing, crying, smiling, dying.

On and on and deeper in he walked.

◖ I'll Spend It With You

THE COUPLE SAT in two wooden chairs in the dark room for a while, listening to the soft crunch of the fire. The tension was thick, and so was the watery air, like the soggy walls of the house were emitting some kind of exasperated breath.

"I don't know why you're upset," Kirk said. "You'd do the same if you were me."

They sat quietly. Heavy silence blanketed the room. The fire crackled. A light pop.

"Wouldn't you?" he said.

"I don't know," Tiffany said.

"You don't know?"

"It doesn't matter now, Kirk. Christ."

Crackle.

Kirk stood. He crossed over to the window and looked outside. He didn't know what he was seeing, and he supposed it didn't matter. A soup of disoriented colors in the sky, reflecting off the shiny black gravel—that was the best way he could describe it. He heard someone laughing outside. The sound sent chills up his spine. Who could laugh in this place? He shuddered.

"Do you want to eat?" he said, his face reflected in the glass.

"You can't pretend this is okay," she said. "Can we even eat here?"

Her question made him start; they'd been here nearly two full days and neither of them had thought about food until now. "I don't know, but we can try."

She grunted. "No, thanks."

Kirk turned in haste and knelt beside her. "Tiffany, please. Try to relax."

She nodded. She took a deep breath and let down her shoulders. Then she began to cry. "I'm so sorry," she wept. *"I'm so sorry."*

"Hey, hey," he said. "It's okay. It was a mistake. *I get it.*"

Tiffany squeezed his hand. "Thank you for coming," she said.

Kirk smiled. "How could I not?"

She tried to smile but it looked more pained than sincere. She stood and grabbed a broom leaning in the corner of the room. It was cracked at the middle of the handle and taped up poorly, but the rest of it was still intact.

"I'm going to tidy up a bit," she said. "This place is a mess."

Kirk nodded, examining the chalky, dusty floor, and smiled at her encouragingly.

Tiffany shuffled a slow dance around the room, sweeping, the broom's bristles hissing over the floor.

Kirk stood and walked to the front door, looking over his shoulder. "I'm going outside for a minute," he said.

"Be careful."

"Yeah."

Kirk opened the door, walked the few steps to the mailbox, and felt his skin bake beneath the heat. *I made the right choice,* he thought.

He looked in the mailbox and found a white envelope. He ripped it open. He pulled out the letter and unfolded it, and read:

A HEARING FOR KIRK AND TIFFANY STONE WILL BE HELD AT 9:00 P.M. AT THE JUSTICE CENTER. PLEASE DON'T BE LATE, AS THERE WILL BE NO RESCHEDULING PERMITTED. THANK YOU.

—INFORMATION CENTER

Kirk brought the note inside and placed it on the red table.

Tiffany was nearly finished sweeping. "What is it?" she asked.

Kirk sighed. "Our hearing."

"When is it?"

"In an hour. That letter must have been in the box all day."

Tiffany's face became a mask of sadness. "Will we make it on time?"

"We have to," Kirk said. "Come on, let's get ready."

Tiffany unlinked her white-gold necklace and cupped it into Kirk's breast pocket. It was a gift he'd given her two years ago, marking their tenth anniversary.

"What—" he started.

"Just hold it for me," she said, and Kirk didn't know why.

They heard a chilling scream outside. Then a woman crying. They ignored it. Kirk adjusted his red tie, and Tiffany helped smooth out his collar.

"You look nice," she said.

"You, too." Kirk smiled.

He kissed her, and felt her creamy lips against his mouth, filling his heart with something like fire and dripping ice. He embraced her, held her there in his arms.

"I love you."

"I love you, too."

They locked the house, wondering if they'd ever return.

"It's so hot," Tiffany said.

"Yeah."

Tiffany frowned and reached for his hand. He took hers as they walked along the gravel path. There was murky darkness hovering all around them.

They could hear the screams and cries more clearly now, but they didn't see their source.

"Maybe you should cover your ears," Kirk said.

She shook her head. "I'm okay."

Kirk knew she was lying because she looked down when she said it. From their years of marriage, he was able to pick up on those signs, those indications. He only wished that he could have been there to pick up on the particular red alarm that would have kept them from this fate—to have stopped her in time.

As if reading his mind, Tiffany gave Kirk's hand a tender squeeze. A moment later, she asked, "Is that it?"

Before them, a gigantic gray structure loomed over the black-paved street. There was some sort of seal on the doors, but nowhere did it say *Justice Center.* Kirk looked around and saw no other buildings—and that soupy sky seemed to be expanding now, frothing and bubbling up nearer to them—so he hurried to the large door.

They walked inside the building. It did look like a courthouse. *Good,* Kirk thought. If they had been late, they would have had problems. They had enough problems already.

"My name is Kirk Stone," he said to the woman at the front desk. "And this is Tiffany Stone, my wife. We have an appointment at nine."

The woman smiled. "Room Three, please."

Kirk felt the reality of it all sink in. He breathed out, and it felt as if his sanity was held in place with the frailty of a gossamer web. The walk had been horrifying. Tiffany must have been equally terrified, if not more so. He could tell by the way her eyes were transfixed ahead of her at nothing in particular.

Justice Room 3 was in black above the door.

"This is it," he said.

"I'm so scared," she said.

He turned to look her in the eyes. "I'll be here." He kissed her. The thought that it might be the last time they kissed made him quiver. He felt his stomach turn as if boiling in a pool of acid. His heart bounced.

He opened the door.

The court room was like the ones they'd seen on television—rows of benches, like pews in a church, the judge's bench elevated above everything else, the jury box, and the stand for witnesses. The room was completely empty.

Kirk and Tiffany sat at their station.

"Do we just wait?" Tiffany asked.

As if on cue, the judge came out of his quarters and walked over to the bench. He sat down and stared at them. He was wearing a black tunic with a black hood over his head. He had a weedy white beard and black eyes. When Kirk glanced over, there was suddenly a jury, every seat occupied. They all wore plastic-looking smiles on their faces.

"Let the hearing for Kirk and Tiffany Stone commence," the judge said in a husky voice.

The room was quiet as the judge shuffled through his papers. He put on thin glasses and pushed the bridge up the slope of his thin nose.

"Tiffany Stone committed an invalid act on June the second," the judge said. "An act unforgivable, which merits dire consequences. Do you remember?"

They both nodded. Tiffany gripped Kirk's hand.

"Let go of his hand," the judge ordered.

Tiffany did. Kirk looked at her sadly.

"Kirk Stone committed no such act and has chosen to be here on his wife's behalf. His presence here is not required. Do you understand this, Mr. Stone?"

"Yes," Kirk said.

"You can leave here whenever you want."

"I understand."

The judge studied him carefully, and then said, "Very well. On June the second, Tiffany committed an act of substance abuse, taking an overdose of sleeping pills while you, Kirk, were in a coma at First Baptist Memorial Hospital. Do you know all this?"

"Yes," he said.

"Tiffany overdosed and was found dead in your apartment that evening. Having no family decision-maker remaining, and considering that you had been in a coma for nearly four months and were showing no signs of recovery, the hospital's ethics committee chose to pull the plug, killing you. Do you understand?"

"I do."

Tiffany's eyes were brimming with tears. She started to reach for Kirk's hand, but apparently remembering what the judge had said before, she pulled back.

"Do you also understand that if your wife would have stayed alive and by your side, you would have awoken three weeks later, perfectly healthy?"

"I understand, Your Honor."

"Very well," the judge said. "For her act, Tiffany Stone has been sentenced to an eternity in Hell. You, however, Mr. Stone, are free to pass through Heaven's gates."

Tiffany broke down then. Tears ran in rivulets from her eyes and she began to groan loudly. Kirk gripped her hand, not caring what the judge thought of it. Her hand was sweating and shaking.

Kirk tried his best to straighten up. "I requested in my first letter that I join her. I thought that's what this hearing was about."

The judge shook his head. "I'm sorry, Mr. Stone, but that won't be possible. We work under very strict conditions. We can't allow someone innocent to go into Hell, even at his own request."

"But I'm a sinner, too," Kirk said. "I'm not innocent."

"I'm sorry, Mr. Stone. This is different."

"Please," Kirk said over Tiffany's weeping. "There must be some way. She was suffering. She didn't mean to overdose. I don't *care* if she killed me. *Please*, Your Honor."

"Mr. Stone, I'm sorry." The judge's face was rigid. "It's impossible."

Before Kirk could add anything else, two stone-faced guards appeared at the door and grabbed Tiffany by the arms. She quivered and screamed at their touch. They had to drag her body as she went nearly limp, and Kirk leaped onto the guards. One of them shoved him against one of the pews. He hissed at the pain that shot up his back.

"Kirk! Help me, Kirk!" Tiffany shouted.

Kirk tried to reach her again, but a third guard held him back. "Get off me!" he roared.

Tiffany continued crying out until the closing door cut off her voice.

Kirk felt his sanity crumble.

"Kirk," the judge said behind him. He was still seated at his bench. *"Kirk,"* he said again.

Kirk Stone turned. His eyes were glazed over, filled with tears, his mouth agape.

"You have to leave, Kirk. You have to go to your own destination now."

"Where are they taking her?" he asked.

Kirk thought for a moment that the judge hadn't heard him, as he gathered files into a pile. Then the judge answered, "You know where."

The guards gripped Kirk's arms and walked him out of the room. He felt lifeless and weak, his feet tripping over the tiles. He saw his tears land on the floor as his feet stepped over them. Before he realized it, he was escorted past the house where he and Tiffany had spent the last two days waiting for their court hearing.

His mind went back to the conversation they'd had two days before, when they had first died. When they had first discovered their fates.

"I'll go to Hell with you," Kirk had said. "I'll tell the judge that. He'll understand."

"You can't!" Tiffany had cried. "I won't let you do that!"

"I can't live without you."

"I can't, either," she'd wept. "But I can't do that to you. Not for eternity."

"It's better than an eternity without you, Tiffany," Kirk had said. "I'll spend it with you, even in Hell."

"Do you think they'd even let you?"

"They have to."

They have to. The words echoed in his mind. Haunting him. Taunting him. Where was she now? *Jesus,* he thought in despair. *Where is she now?*

He started to feel his memories of her slipping away. Their wedding day, the day they met—he suddenly couldn't remember any of it. Did the bastards have to take that away, too?

The guards finally released his arms. He stood in front of a golden road, the gate to Heaven before him, large and intimidating. Kirk looked back at the guards, who had already begun their trek back to the Justice Center.

"Hey," Kirk called out, thin films of dry tears on his face.

The guards turned.

"Are you positive—and I mean *positive*—that there's no way for me to be with my wife?"

The guards looked at each other and then looked back at Kirk. "You don't have a wife," one of the guards said.

Kirk tried his very hardest—God, did he try—to remember. Tiff . . . Ti . . . *Damn, what was her name?*

"That's right," he mumbled, his eyebrows furrowed. "I don't have a wife."

The guards turned again and walked off. Kirk watched them until they disappeared into a dark tunnel. He turned again to face the gates.

He pushed one side of the gate, and it opened with ease.

It occurred to him that he should leave his possessions behind. The thought came suddenly, as if planted by a foreign influence. He searched his pockets and found only a white-gold necklace in his breast pocket.

He didn't recognize it. Puzzled, he set it on the ground. Then he stepped in.

The gates closed behind him.

BENJAMIN CARD was born and raised in Miami, FL and is twenty-four years old. He is the youngest of four brothers and has been creating fiction since his elementary school days, when he and his older brother Abraham would hold contests at their father's furniture shop to see which of them could fabricate a better comic book. Though those early writings were just meant to kill time, they also sparked Benjamin's fascination with science fiction, fantasy, and horror.

Benjamin is also the founder of the band My Flesh Heart, which currently has two albums for sale on iTunes and other leading music websites. Card still resides in South Florida.

Follow Benjamin Card on Vine, Twitter, and Instagram by searching his name. If you enjoyed this book, please leave a review on Goodreads.com, BN.com, or Amazon.com.

Did you enjoy the book?

We welcome all feedback and queries.
Villipede.com

DARKNESS AD INFINITUM

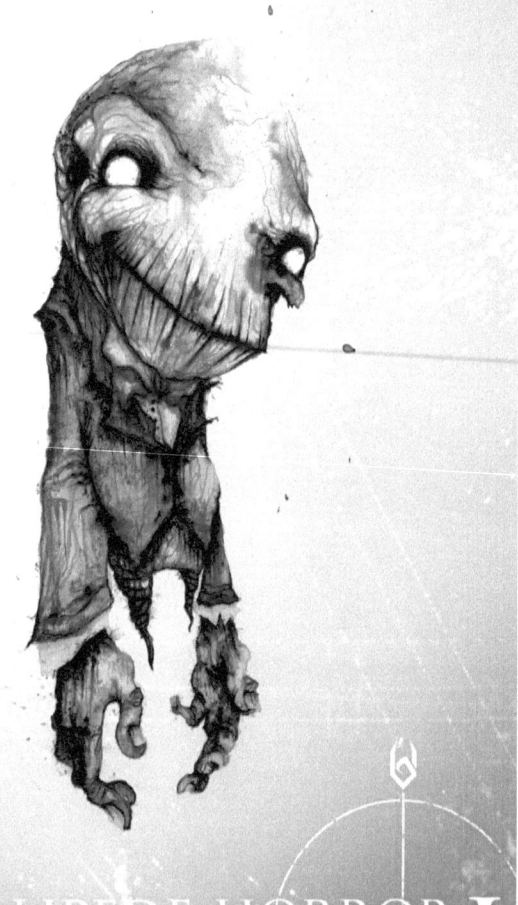

VILLIPEDE HORROR
ANTHOLOGY I

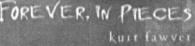
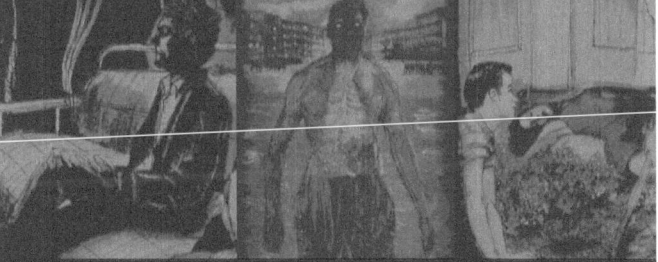

J. DANIEL STONE

THE ABSENCE of LIGHT

"**THE WORLD NEEDS GOTH BOYS AND GIRLS**—WHO BETTER TO GUIDE A READER INTO A GOOD GHOST STORY LIKE THAT OF A BLACK-CLAD BEARER OF ANGST AND PAIN?

J. DANIEL STONE'S *THE ABSENCE OF LIGHT* OFFERS A HORDE OF SUCH MORBID YOUTH AS WELL AS SATISFYING HAUNTS."

—STEVE BERMAN
OWNER/FOUNDER OF LETHE PRESS

Villipede.com

THE GLASS PARACHUTE

villipede
publications

SF

anthology 1

alex j. kane

martin l. shoemaker

david tallerman

s.c. wade

grayson bray morris

matt edginton

ben godby

jasmine michaelson

rob oxley

"Reading this collection gave me some serious flashbacks to the joys of being a young, teenage geek whose greatest pleasure was curling up with a science fiction anthology on a lazy Sunday afternoon and completely disappearing into another world"

— Bryant Dillon, Fanboy Comics President